Gothic Originals

Gothic Originals

Published so far
Charlotte Dacre, *The Passions* (1811), edited by Jennifer Airey
Elizabeth Gunning, *The Foresters. A Novel* (1796), edited by Valerie Grace Derbyshire
Dion Boucicault, *The Vampire* (1852) and *The Phantom* (1873), edited by Matthew Knight and Gary D. Rhodes

In preparation
The Female Vampire in Hispanic Fiction, edited by Megan DeVirgilis
Mary Elizabeth Braddon, *The Factory Girl* (1863), edited by Bridget Marshall
Washington Allston, *Monaldi: A Tale* (1841), edited by Kerry Dean Carso

Gothic Originals

Dion Boucicault

The Vampire
(1852)

The Phantom
(1873)

Gothic Originals

With full introductions and explanatory notes to the text, Gothic Originals *consists of scholarly editions aimed at readers, teachers and students of the gothic. Each text is a definitive scholarly edition, edited by an expert in their field. The series consists of texts from the eighteenth century onwards, and includes hidden classics to forgotten anthologies of terror. The series is an essential collection for any serious scholar of the gothic.*

General Editor
Anthony Mandal, *Cardiff University*

Series Editor
Andrew Smith, *University of Sheffield*

Editorial Board
Carol Margaret Davison, *University of Windsor*
Jerrold E. Hogle, *University of Arizona*
Marie Mulvey-Roberts, *University of the West of England*
Franz Potter, *National University*
Laurence Talairach, *University of Toulouse Jean Jaurès*
Dale Townshend, *Manchester Metropolitan University*
Lisa Vargo, *University of Saskatchewan*
Angela Wright, *University of Sheffield*

Dion Boucicault

The Vampire
The Phantom

edited by Matthew Knight and Gary D. Rhodes

UNIVERSITY OF WALES PRESS
CARDIFF
2024

© Matthew Knight and Gary D. Rhodes, 2024

Typeset in Minion 3 and SchwarzKopf New
at the Centre for Editorial and Intertextual Research, Cardiff University.

All rights reserved. No part of this book may be reproduced in any material form (including photocopying or storing it in any medium by electronic means and whether or not transiently or incidentally to some other use of this publication) without the written permission of the copyright owner. Applications for the copyright owner's written permission to reproduce any part of this publication should be addressed to the University of Wales Press, University Registry, King Edward VII Avenue, Cardiff CF10 3NS.

www.uwp.co.uk

British Library CIP Data
A catalogue record for this book is available from the British Library.

ISBN 978-1-83772-150-4 (hardback)
       978-1-83772-151-1 (ePDF)
       978-1-83772-152-8 (ePUB)

The right of Matthew Knight and Gary D. Rhodes to be identified as Editors of this work has been asserted in accordance with sections 77 and 79 of the Copyright, Designs and Patents Act 1988.

Contents

Acknowledgements ix
List of Illustrations x
Introduction xi
   The Vampire xiii
   The Phantom xvii
   Conclusion xxiii
   Select Bibliography xxvii
Note on the Texts xxviii
   The Vampire xxviii
   The Phantom xxviii
   The Present Edition xxix
   Abbreviated Stage Directions xxx

THE VAMPIRE, A PHANTASM IN THREE DRAMAS
The First Drama—Raby Castle 1
   Characters in the First Drama 4
   Scene One 5
   Scene Two 12
   Scene Three 22
The Second Drama—Raby Hall 25
   Characters in the Second Drama 24
The Third Drama 39
   Characters in the Third Drama 40
   Scene One 41
   Scene Two 47
   Scene Three 52
   Scene Four 56

THE PHANTOM, A PLAY IN TWO ACTS
Act One 60
   Characters in Act One, Period 1645 60
   Scene One 61
   Scene Two 66
   Scene Three 75
   Scene Four 76
Act Two 78
   Characters in Act Two 78
   Scene One 79

CONTENTS

Scene Two. 87
Scene Three 90
Scene Four 94
Emendation List 97
   The Vampire. 98
   The Phantom 99
Explanatory Notes. 101
   The Vampire. 101
   The Phantom 108

Acknowledgements

THE EDITORS WOULD LIKE TO THANK THE FOLLOWING PERSONS for their kind assistance: Kristin Dewey, Sarah Lewis, Don and Phyllis Rhodes, Jennifer Knight, Oisín and Rosalie Knight, Robert L. Singer, Richard Schmidt, Sandra Law, Elizabeth Ricketts-Jones, LeEtta Schmidt, Amanda Boczar and Sydney Jordan. The editors would also like to express their deepest appreciation to the following institutions: University of Wales Press, University of South Florida Libraries Special Collections, the Billy Rose Theatre Division of the New York Public Library and the University of South Florida Libraries Interlibrary Loan Department.

List of Illustrations

Frontispiece. Artwork of Boucicault's *The Phantom*, *Frank Leslie's Illustrated Newspaper*, 26 July 1856 x

Figure 1. First page of Boucicault's handwritten manuscript of *The Vampire* (MS-V) 3
    Courtesy University of South Florida Libraries Special
    Collections, Dion Boucicault Theatre Collection

Figure 2. Boucicault's sketch of the stage design for the Second Drama in *The Vampire* (MS-V) 23
    Courtesy University of South Florida Libraries Special
    Collections, Dion Boucicault Theatre Collection

Figure 3. First page of Act II of Boucicault's 1852 script for *The Phantom* (MS-P) 58
    Courtesy University of South Florida Libraries Special
    Collections, Dion Boucicault Theatre Collection

Introduction

> I have followed public taste; I have not led it.
> — *Dion Boucicault*[1]

DURING THE YEARS 1840–1880, DION BOUCICAULT (1820–1890) was perhaps the most prominent and prolific dramatist on the world stage, popular with international audiences and adored by Queen Victoria.[2] In addition to writing or adapting more than two hundred plays, Boucicault proved himself to be an accomplished actor and director. He established the royalty system for the payment of playwrights, inaugurated an American school of acting, counted fireproof scenery among his many stagecraft innovations and successfully lobbied the US Congress for copyright legislation for playwrights in 1856.

Born Dionysius Lardner Boursiquot in Dublin in December 1820, Boucicault grew up ashamed that his legitimate father was likely not his mother's husband, the wine merchant Samuel Boursiquot, but rather Dionysius Lardner, an academic and encyclopaedist. But this indignity did not prevent him from accepting Lardner's quarterly allowances to pursue his education and acting career in England. Boucicault was a driven young man, making his stage debut before his eighteenth birthday. A case of mistaken identity resulted in a commission to write a five-act comedy for Covent Garden, which he completed in thirty days. On 4 March 1841, *London Assurance* made its debut to a packed house and rave reviews.[3] At the age of twenty, Dion Boucicault became, as Deirdre McFeely has observed, 'the sensation of the London stage, a position he would hold on and off over the next forty years'.[4]

Boucicault positioned himself in the spotlight over the next decade, courting scandal and delivering successful dramas to an appreciative public. His marriage to a wealthy and much older French widow raised eyebrows. Her mysterious death in 1848, coupled with his silence on the matter, provided fodder for gossip columns and made him even more of a star. Boucicault's reputation as a master of stagecraft, dialogue, adaptation and self-promotion flourished.[5]

The year 1852 was pivotal for the 31-year-old Boucicault. His new play *The Corsican Brothers* became the runaway hit of the season. Theatres worldwide adopted the 'Corsican Trap' he designed for the play. Then, he portrayed the title character of his three-act drama *The Vampire*. Though he earned rave reviews for his acting, most critics and audiences believed the play was mediocre. He also married the beautiful and talented actress Agnes Robertson, who co-starred with him in *The Vampire*. Owing to interpersonal trouble with his theatre patron, professional restlessness and his desire to become an international celebrity, Boucicault and his new bride decided to move to the United States.[6]

After the disappointing reception of *The Vampire* in London, Boucicault realized that audiences likely wanted less challenging material. They wanted more realism and comedy, and so he shortened *The Vampire* to two acts, added episodes of ethnic humour and eliminated numerous characters, the result becoming *The Phantom*, a considerably different play.[7] The move was wise and profitable: soon, his career and reputation in America soared. By Boucicault's own admission, however, his plays were not of the highest literary quality, as he wrote for an unsophisticated audience. He once famously said, 'I can spin out these rough and tumble dramas as a hen lays eggs. It's a degrading occupation, but more money has been made out of guano than of poetry'.[8] If a play did not get a positive response from the audience, Boucicault would alter it to garner public favour; if the public thought a tragedy had too unhappy an ending, he would temper it at the next performance.

Boucicault continued to churn out period-piece melodramas for decades, with as many people eager to see their sensation scenes as the plays themselves. After opening in London in 1860, *The Colleen Bawn* enjoyed the longest run in British theatre history, leading Boucicault to create a touring company to ensure the play's quality wherever it ran.[9] Other 'Irish' plays like *Arrah-na-Pogue* (1864) and *The Shaughraun* (1874) cemented Boucicault's international reputation. During the 1870s, it was common for dozens of his plays to be running in the United Kingdom, the United States and Australia. Boucicault won and squandered fortunes, delighted in his wars of words in the press and enjoyed being an international celebrity. But for all his theatrical knowledge, he failed to observe that the public were growing tired of his style of melodrama. And so, by the 1880s, he was something of a broken man. The press was unforgiving in their treatment of his new plays. Even worse, the public remained indifferent. Boucicault discovered too late his error in seeking immediate fame over lasting literary distinction. Only two weeks before died, heartbroken, he wrote to a friend: 'It has been a long jig and I am beginning to see the pathos of it. I have written for a monster who forgets'.[10]

Perhaps no two plays illustrate Dion Boucicault's propensity to alter his work at the behest of public opinion better than *The Vampire* and *The Phantom*. The latter play underwent numerous revisions after being published by Samuel French in 1856, while the former has languished in relative obscurity, with no published edition or critical commentary for more than 170 years.[11] Fortunately, Boucicault kept his original draft scripts for both vampire plays, and they now form a part of the Dion Boucicault Theatre Collection at the University of South Florida (USF) Libraries in Tampa.[12] These manuscripts, in consultation with published and archival resources, provided the basis for this first full edition of Boucicault's innovative *tour de force*, *The Vampire*. His manuscripts also have allowed this volume to feature his revised version of *The Phantom* (produced in 1873) that differs considerably from the existing Samuel French edition of 1856.

THE VAMPIRE

As detailed in the Note on the Texts, pp. xxviii and xxix–xxx, this edition of Boucicault's *The Vampire* is compiled from three unpublished sources, all prepared in 1852: a holograph manuscript, a handwritten script and a handwritten prompt book. Boucicault purportedly wrote the original manuscript in six days and, as was his practice, relied on previously published source material.[13] For example, he drew heavily upon *Le Vampire* by Alexandre Dumas *père*, which had premiered in Paris on 20 December 1851. At times Boucicault's version follows the plot in parallel.[14] Demonstrating his familiarity with published vampire lore as well as stage representations, Boucicault also drew upon John Polidori's 1819 short story *The Vampyre* (moonlight's rejuvenating power on a mortally wounded vampire, the blood oath); James Malcolm Rymer's 1845–1847 penny dreadful *Varney the Vampyre* (the vampire's garb, evocative portraits, a focus on Oliver Cromwell); and James Robinson Planché's 1820 play *The Vampire: Or the Bride of the Isles* (the vampire's psychic power over his victims).[15] That said, Boucicault importantly added his own stylistic touches and innovations, notably adapting Dumas *père*'s tapestry sequence by replacing its fairies and ghouls with portraits that come to life and emerge from their frames to warn of impending danger.[16] Boucicault also became the first to write, direct and perform the role of a vampire on stage.[17]

The structure of *The Vampire* is ingenious: beginning in the year 1660, each act takes place exactly one century after the other, and the characters in Acts II and III are direct descendants of those in the first. This framing places the final act in 1860, eight years in the future for those who attended the Royal Princess's Theatre in 1852. The play opens in the village of Raby Peveryl in North Wales in 1660. Oliver Cromwell has just died and, as villagers celebrate the restoration of Charles II and the monarchy, a stranger named Lucy Peveryl arrives looking for a guide to Raby Castle. But the castle is cursed: Alan Raby, a Cromwell supporter, had murdered his two Royalist brothers before a group of Cavaliers hurled him from a castle turret. For his crimes, the earth refused to accept Raby's body, forcing him to wander the earth as a vampire. Every one hundred years, on August 15th, Raby must take the life of a young woman so that he might live another century. Watkyn Rhys, a local resident, reluctantly leads Lucy and a group of supporters up the dangerous passes of Snowdon (Yr Wyddfa) to the castle. Lucy and her fiancé Roland are murdered by Raby, but he himself is shot through the heart. Before he dies, he entreats his killer to take him to the peaks of Snowdon at midnight, where he is rejuvenated by the rays of the moon.

INTRODUCTION

The second act parallels the first, this time taking place inside the halls of Raby Castle in 1760. Hanging in the chamber where Alan Raby was first murdered are portraits of his victims of the previous century: his two brothers, Lucy and Roland. A fourth painting hangs under a black curtain, which is later revealed to be a sketch made of Raby the night Lucy was murdered in 1660. Alice Peveryl is awaiting the return of her brother Edgar, who has been traveling with one Gervase Rookwood—a sobriquet for Alan Raby himself. Watty Rees, a descendent of Watkyn, recognizes Raby and tries to warn Alice. Lady Peveryl, however, is seduced by Raby, who begins to wield power over her. In an incredible scene, Alice falls asleep and the portraits come to life, with Lucy warning her of the peril in the castle. Just as Alice unveils the hidden portrait to reveal the vampire's likeness, Raby appears and murders her as the clock strikes midnight. As Edgar arrives to avenge her death, Raby places a hand on his head and kills him with his psychic powers. As in Act 1, the vampire is granted one hundred more years of life.

The final act is again set a century later, on 15 August 1860. Walter Rees, descendent of Watty and Watkyn, is a lawyer in search of his cousin Ada. One Gervase Rookwood has her under his spell, however, and here Boucicault displays more of the mesmerizing power of Alan Raby. When he is close, Ada cannot resist him, even calling him her 'master'; but she regains some of her senses when he is at a distance. Before Raby can make Ada his latest victim and claim another one hundred years of life, Rees discovers ancient documents revealing Raby's identity and sets the clocks back one hour, thereby thwarting the vampire's sinister devices. In the final scene atop Snowdon, Raby is defeated, with his first female victim, Lucy Peveryl, pulling him down into the earth.

Boucicault likely based Alan Raby on previous vampire characterizations, but he imbued the role with an intensity and seductive charm that captivated his audiences.[18] Raby is as much a mesmerist as a bloodthirsty fiend, and, like Dracula, he exerts mental control over his victims.[19] As Roxana Stuart has noted, Boucicault also adds a note of religious mania to Alan Raby, which appears to be a veiled attack on organized religion and the power of zealots to control vulnerable minds.[20] Aside from his Puritan extremism, Boucicault may have intentionally stressed Raby's connection to Oliver Cromwell to evoke the common motif in Irish folklore of Cromwell as a demon, an arch-villain, and even as a vampire-like creature whose corpse was rejected by Irish soil.[21] Given his Irish background, the choice of Wales for the setting of The Vampire may seem surprising, but the romanticism of the Welsh countryside and the majesty of Snowdon likely contributed to his decision.

The Vampire in England

Despite the innovations of stagecraft and composition, as well as of Boucicault's mesmerizing performance as Alan Raby, the British public were reluctant to embrace the play. Vampires were hardly forgotten in 1852 when Boucicault's play premiered, including the specific undead that inspired him.

In March of that year, for example, London's Theatre Royal staged Planché's *The Vampire; or, The Bride of the Isles*.[22] Manchester's Theatre Royal staged it that same month.[23] And in April and May 1852, the publishing firm Colburn & Company advertised Polidori's *The Vampire* for sale in a 'cheap' edition; the publisher attributed it to Lord Byron, the longstanding authorial error continuing, perhaps intentionally.[24] While this entertainment could have been perceived as competition, it also might have helped Boucicault, evidence that the public hungered for vampires.

On 14 June 1852, Boucicault's *The Vampire, a Phantasm, Related in Three Dramas* (as advertisements called it) premiered at the Royal Princess's Theatre on a double bill with George William Lovell's five-act play *The Trial of Love*. Opening night was a benefit performance for Charles Kean, the actor famed for his Shakespearean revivals. Kean was also stage manager for the Royal Princess's between 1850 and 1859. Townsend Walsh wrote, 'Kean deemed "vampires" beneath his tragic dignity, so Boucicault himself appeared as the supernatural creature.'[25] The vampire role marked Boucicault's debut on the London stage, at least using the Dion Boucicault name.[26]

The London *Morning Chronicle* was particularly impressed with *The Vampire*, publishing the most favourable review the drama received:

> [T]he recent reputation of the Princess's for ghost dramas naturally quickened the public curiosity. The result was that the curtain rose upon a very excited and eager house-ful [*sic*] of spectators. [...] [Boucicault's] play in its treatment is perfectly original and has nothing to do with Dumas' late drama on the subject. [...] His make-up in the three phases was each in its way admirable. The intense pallor of the countenance, showing the glitter of the eye and the blackness of the peculiarly cut hair, was preserved throughout. [...] The play was splendidly put on the stage.[27]

Another London newspaper, the *Morning Post*, also expressed admiration for the play, drawing particular attention to Boucicault's acting:

> Though we cannot but find fault with this grotesque phantasm, it is impossible to speak in too high terms of the diction, the acting, and the *mise en scène*. Of Mr. Boucicault's histrionic powers, we have to record our most favourable opinion. His carriage is graceful, his manner impressive, and his voice finely toned.[28]

Rather than cite previous vampire plays, the *Morning Post* believed *The Vampire* was an adaptation of Charles Maturin's *Melmoth the Wanderer* (1820).

Reynolds's Newspaper obliquely noted Boucicault's stage predecessors as well as the inspiration of Gothic literature:

> The plot of the play rests on a superstition, not unfamiliar to the stage, or readers of works issuing from the once-famed Minerva press.[29] [...] The scenery is very fine, particularly a representation of the vampire's corpse stretched upon the hills in the pale moonlight, and its ghastly revivification: the terminating spectral scene is one of magnificent horror. But in spite of admirable scenic effect, [and] capital acting on the part of Mr. Boucicault, whose appearance and tone of voice were for the occasion cleverly adapted to the character, the

piece, which is powerfully written, can scarcely be said to have met with that success we are so accustomed to record of the productions at this house. At its conclusion, however, the author was loudly applauded.[30]

While the London *Observer* complained that *The Vampire*'s 'accumulation of horrors becomes somewhat wearisome in the end', its critic also drew attention to Boucicault's performance:

> Mr. Boucicault's success as an actor in this part was almost complete. His figure is slight and not inelegant; his features regular, his eye is quick, and its expression capable of some dramatic intensity. His voice is also well fitted for the stage; it is clear, distinct, and not unmanly in its tones; while his elocution and pronunciation, with perhaps the exception of a slight Irish brogue in the more empathetic passages, are distinguished by a good intonation and just emphasis.[31]

The Times of London was equally unimpressed by the play, but nevertheless spoke highly of Boucicault:

> The success of Mr. Boucicault as an actor—for he made his debut as the Vampire—was far more unequivocal than that of the piece. The attitudes were well studied, the chilly aspect was carefully made up, and the few words of dialogue were judiciously spoken, so that throughout the whole piece he fully preserved his supernatural distinctiveness.[32]

The reviewer noted the applause given to Boucicault but added that 'several of the audience evinced displeasure when the shroud-clad Lucy and Alice showed their grim figures in the moonlight.'[33]

Henry Morley of the London *Examiner* was even less enthused, his review being often quoted by future authors, perhaps because Morley included it in his 1891 collection of theatre criticism:[34]

> If there is truth in the old adage, that 'when things are at the worst they must mend', the amelioration of Spectral Melodrama is not distant; for it has reached the extreme point of inanity in [...] *The Vampire*. Its plot is chiefly copied from a piece which some years ago turned the Lyceum into a Chamber of Horrors. [...] [T]he dreary repetition of fantastical horror almost exhausted even the patience which a benefit enjoins. Unfortunately the mischief of such a piece, produced at a respectable theatre, does not end with the weariness of the spectators, who come to shudder and remain to yawn; for it is not only beside 'the purpose of playing,' but directly contravenes it; and, though it may be too dull to pervert the tastes of those who witness its vapid extravagances, it has power to bring discredit on the most genial of arts.[35]

Lloyd's Weekly Newspaper was even harsher, telling readers: 'we have seldom met anything on the stage more abounding in pure unalloyed, undefecated absurdity than *The Vampire*', adding that Boucicault's acting was 'not above mediocrity.'[36]

And yet, some audience members clearly enjoyed *The Vampire*, even if they were in the minority. Queen Victoria became the play's most notable admirer, seeing it on opening night with Prince Albert and declaring, 'Mr. Boucicault, who is very handsome and has a fine voice, acted very impressively. I can never forget his livid face and fixed look, in the first two Dramas. It quite haunts me.'[37] She even commissioned a portrait of him in the vampire role. That said, she was less thrilled after watching the play again: 'It does not bear seeing a second time, and is, in fact, very trashy.'[38] Whether her opinion changed organically or because of negative critical reception is difficult to say.

At any rate, *The Vampire* ended its one-month run at the Royal Princess's on 14 July 1852, the theatre then closing its season for the summer. The following day, the Olympic Theatre staged Planché's *The Vampire; or, the Bride of the Isles* on a double bill with *Abelard and Heloise*. Observing its similarity to Boucicault's play, *Reynolds's Newspaper* told readers that the Planché had been 'well received and will probably enjoy a respectable run.'[39] The Olympic's decision to stage Planché was likely motivated by Boucicault's vampire.

To be sure, vampires had their place in the London theatre in 1852, but certainly not to the extent Boucicault later recalled. In 1873, he told an interviewer, 'I wrote *The Corsican Brothers, The Phantom*, and a score of others. These were the rage of the day.'[40] *The Vampire* was by no means a failure, but it certainly did not inspire a rage.[41]

THE PHANTOM

In anticipation of his relocation to America, and with hopes of opening *The Vampire* at Wallack's Theatre in New York City, Boucicault sent a complete prompt book to James Wallack in 1852. Given the play's lacklustre response in London and the absence of a commitment from Wallack to produce it, Boucicault streamlined the plot to two acts, enhanced the dialogue and eliminated some of the more elaborate stagecraft. The result was not merely an abbreviated version of *The Vampire*: it was instead a very different play, *The Phantom*. In being condensed to two acts, the structure of *The Phantom* differs considerably from *The Vampire*. While the Puritan Alan Raby returns as the fiend who must feast upon the blood of a maiden before being revived by moonlight, much of the stagecraft wizardry has been removed. Gone are the living portraits in the second act of *The Vampire*, as well as the important role of time and the clock tower. Moreover, Raby is no longer dragged down to hell by one of his earlier victims, but is rather hurled into a chasm where moonlight cannot reach.

The plot and dialogue are also changed to provide more comic relief. In Act I, the newlywed couple Davy and Janet are introduced as rural Welsh innkeepers, sometime around the time of Cromwell's death. The pair engage in mildly sexual banter until, as in *The Vampire*, Lucy Peveryl arrives looking for an escort to Raby Castle. The plot follows in much the same fashion as the first act of The Vampire, although Davy continually shows himself to be a coward, especially when he recognizes Alan Raby in the castle. Otherwise, Act I ends as did *The Vampire*, with Alan Raby killing Lucy and Roland, himself being shot, yet convincing his killer to take him atop Snowdon where he is rejuvenated in the moonlight.

The second act differs drastically from *The Vampire*, with an entirely new set of characters inhabiting Raby Hall roughly a century later.[42] In this act the comic relief is provided by Corporal Stump and the maid Jenny, who are soon to be wed. The main action focuses on Ada Raby, who, upon learning of the death of her sweetheart Edgar while off at war, dies of grief. After lying in a coffin for five days, she is miraculously revived by a stranger named Rookwood, who, as it happens, also brought Edgar back to life on the battlefield in Germany and since returned to Raby Castle to lay claim on the property through an ancient deed. Rookwood, as before, is none other than Alan Raby. Ada is helpless to withstand Raby's power, and he plans to marry her in exchange for relinquishing his claims on the castle. Edgar returns to fight for Ada's love, but the power of the vampire is too strong. Only by realizing that Rookwood forged the property deed is the physician and scholar of the dark arts Dr Rees able to thwart Alan Raby. After consulting his trusted book of necromancy, Rees has Stump shoot Raby through the heart and, before he can rejuvenate in the moonlight, throws him into an abyss.

This new, vastly altered version of *The Vampire* was published by Samuel French in 1856, and contains less than ten per cent of the dialogue from *The Vampire*.[43] The text of *The Phantom* included in the present volume emerged from research into four unpublished sources (see the Note on the Texts, pp. xxviii–xxx for fuller details). Three of these sources, all watermarked 1852 form the core of the Samuel French edition of 1856, while the present edition is based on the fourth, undated source: a handwritten prompt book most likely produced for a short one-week run at McVicker's Theatre in Chicago beginning 27 January 1873.[44] *The Phantom* of 1873 differs considerably from the Samuel French version of 1856, particularly in its pacing and minor character development. The entire subplot of Davy and Janet's nuptials is excised, although much of the plot remains the same for the remainder of Act I. The next act also removes a subplot of planned marriages, with Stump and Jenny acting more as accomplices than comic relief. The relationship between Raby and Ada is heightened in this version, and his magnetic hold over her feels more powerful given the absence of comedic subplot. Overall, it seems Boucicault knew his 1873 audience well: they preferred more spectacle and less farcical distraction.

In a two-page summary of his 1873 production found in PB-P (printed in part by the *Chicago Tribune*), Boucicault drafted a bold press announcement: 'The renowned romantic drama the *Phantom*. Note: this weird and emotional story so marvelously executed and realized by Mr. Boucicault is the most intense and original sensation of the modern stage.'[45] Scholars and general readers will learn much about Boucicault's creative process by examining the 1873 script of *The Phantom* included in this volume in relation to the 1856 version.

The Phantom in America
The *Phantom*'s initial public notice in America became phantasmal in its own right. Advertisements claimed that the play would premiere at Boston's National Theatre in September 1854. A newspaper advertisement in the *Boston Post* added an exclamation mark to the title and—with no mention of the title change or narrative alterations—made links to its past on the British stage: 'as portrayed by [Boucicault] and Miss Robertson before Queen Victoria.'[46] For reasons unknown, the new play did not open anywhere in 1854. Its debut would have to wait nearly two years.

With Boucicault and Agnes Robertson playing the lead roles, *The Phantom* opened at the National Theatre in Philadelphia on 12 May 1856. Local publicity falsely claimed that the play was the most successful ever staged at Charles Kean's theatre in London, where it appeared for 'many consecutive months'.[47] Another report incorrectly alleged that Queen Victoria had attended it 'four or five times'.[48] Relying on the then-current American spelling of Boucicault (with an 'r' added), the Philadelphia *Sunday Dispatch* told readers:

> The plot of the piece, or rather the general idea, has undoubtedly been suggested by that awful horror of the melodramatic school, *The Vampire*, which, some years ago, was so popular with novel-reading apprentices and young ladies who adored 'the three Spaniards' and Mrs. Radcliffe. Wherever Mr. Bourcicault got his material for this effort in the spectral line, we must say he has accomplished the consummation devoutly wished for by all dramatists—a drama which has all of the elements to give it popularity. The characters are well drawn, the language is good, and the interest increases and becomes intensely absorbing to the audience, at least that portion of it whose imaginations are so vivid that they forget the existence of such an item as reality.[49]

The favourable review invoked *The Vampire*, but which *Vampire* is difficult to discern. The mention of Radcliffe implies the reference was to Polidori, but it could also have referred to Planché.

Boucicault then staged *The Phantom* at Wallack's Theatre in New York, opening night being 1 July 1856. The *New York Times* incorrectly reported that the performance marked the play's 'first time' in America.[50] The *New York Herald* believed:

> Mr. Bourcicault's 'business,' to use a technical term, was quite effective, and his Phantom was ghostly in the extreme. Miss Robertson and the others were quite good, and one of the best things of the night was the performance of an old doctor by Mr. Burnett, a stranger, we think, to the Metropolitan boards.[51]

Putnam's Monthly Magazine also offered praise, telling readers that *The Phantom* 'possesses a most ghastly fascination'.[52]

By contrast, *The Albion* was as quizzical about Boucicault's reasons for mounting the play as it was its theatrical origins:

> Can you conceive of Mr. Bourcicault who is proverbial for talent and taste, constructing a play out of such materials [as vampires]? I can not and will not. I know the bill says, '*Written* by Dion Bourcicault,' but we all know what that

insignificant phrase 'written' means in connection with [...] our present race of English playwrights. It means Taken from the French. Dozens of plays are 'written' in England every year, but ten out of every dozen are direct, immediate, palpable thefts from France. Before they see daylight in London, they have seen gaslight in Paris. Were I called up to decide on the paternity of *The Phantom*, I should lay it at the door of Dumas.[53]

The Phantom continued playing at Wallack's into the autumn of 1856, the run becoming its most successful in America and leading to the Samuel French edition.

In 1857, *The Phantom* appeared at the Boston Theatre in Boston, and at the Louisville Theatre in Louisville, Kentucky.[54] In 1859, Boucicault staged it at the Washington Theatre in Washington, DC.[55] Years later, the *Evening Star* quoted one audience member recalling how impressed he had been with Boucicault's vampire:

Boucicault presented the character of the phantom in a manner that horrified while it electrified the audience. [...] The presentment of this human nightmare by Mr. Boucicault was most horribly vivid. He appeared on the stage as a sort of living corpse, bloodless and exanimate. So great was the strain of this extraordinary part upon the actor that, after it had been performed for a while in Washington, Mr. Boucicault said to his partner, Mr. Stuart, 'We must take this play off the bills; it is too much for my nerves'.[56]

The same person enthusiastically judged *The Phantom* to be 'perhaps the most remarkable play that Boucicault ever wrote'.[57]

As of 1863, *The Phantom* appeared at Barnum's Museum in New York.[58] That same year, the play also appeared at the New Bowery Theatre, with G. C. Boniface in the lead role and J. W. Lingard (the New Bowery's proprietor) as Dr Rees.[59] *The Phantom* also appeared in Detroit in 1866 with J. S. Edwards as the vampire.[60]

One of *The Phantom*'s most notable post-Wallack's appearance in America came in Chicago, where it opened at McVicker's Theatre on 27 January 1873 and ran for one week. This was the first performance using the amended text of the play found in PB-P and included in this edition. Boucicault and Robertson reprised the lead roles. The *Chicago Times* responded:

The wierd [sic], ghoulish, and altogether unnatural story is very ingeniously adapted, but all of Mr. Boucicault's skill as a writer for the stage, and the feverish excitement which the movement of the plot sometimes tends to create in ill-regulated minds, cannot divest the theme of its unpleasantness. The horrible is not a proper theme for art uses, for the simple reason that it always involves an element of disgust.[61]

The *Chicago Evening Mail* echoed that sentiment, claiming *The Phantom* was 'by no means so pleasing'.[62] The *Chicago Tribune* deemed it 'unworthy' of Boucicault.[63] And the *Inter Ocean* reported, 'the audience did not appear to appreciate this churchyard play as well as they might have done' in eras past.[64] The *Chicago Evening Post* viewed the same content in different terms, praising Boucicault and Robertson, stating, 'The drama cannot fail to be attractive, especially to lovers of the weird and terrible.'[65] Though appreciated by some audiences and at least a few critics, *The Phantom* became no more a rage in America than Boucicault's *The Vampire* had been in London.

The Phantom in England
Determined that he could make vampires popular, Boucicault staged *The Phantom* in London at the Adelphi Theatre, with opening night being 21 April 1862. One journalist reported publicity on a scale later afforded to some twentieth-century horror movies:

> For some weeks past, London has been placarded with great ugly bills, half the size of a house, on which are the ominous words, 'Have you seen the Phantom?' Considering there was no Phantom to be seen, an answer could not well be given in the affirmative; but the idea was to get up a sensation, and induce people to question one another as to the meaning of this extraordinary question.[66]

Another writer noted the posters hanging 'from every wall, from every boarding', thus creating a 'gloomy curiosity.'[67]

Such publicity seems to have worked, as the audience assembled for the premiere was large.[68] The London *Observer* explained that Boucicault wrote *The Phantom*:

> upon the basis of a [Planché] melodrama called *The Vampire*, which playgoers of a certain date will remember by its connection with Mr. T. P. Cooke in his younger days. The modern piece is by no means so good as the elder, but its dramatic poverty, disagreeableness, and intense absurdity are, to a certain extent, compensated for by the two principal scenes—a ruined castle and the peak of Ben Nevis—which do great credit to the pencil of Mr. Telbin. Both are seen under the effects of moonlight, and both belong to that class of scenic illustration so successfully carried out by Mr. William Beverley, in which the notion of a solid reality is communicated by elaborately built 'sets'. The beauty of these two scenes, in all probability, prevented the aversion of the audience to the piece itself being expressed in stronger terms than it was.[69]

The *Observer* review did not mention Boucicault's own version of *The Vampire* in 1852, but did levy attention on his performance:

> Mr. Boucicault, as usual, is his own actor. A contemporary alleges, perhaps upon authority, that he 'makes up his head into a semblance of Lord Byron', from some presumed identification of the story with the well-known fragment attributed to the noble poet, but the similitude, we confess, did not strike us. Mr. Boucicault, however, carried out his own ideal very ably, and the pallid face, noiseless step, and impassive manner of the gentleman demon, produced a sort of supernatural presence which was by no means inartistic, and to which the cold steadiness of gaze, half mournful and half malign, with which he has surveyed his intended victim lent additional impressiveness.[70]

A critic for the London *Standard* also drew attention to *The Phantom*'s past, reminding readers of T. P. Cooke starring in Planché's play at the English Opera House in 1820:

> We will at once say that we prefer Planché to Boucicault. *The Vampire* is more natural, if we may apply such a phrase to a drama of this kind, than *The Phantom*, and the Vampire, although he is a vampire, is a much pleasanter personage in every respect in the old drama than he is in Mr. Boucicault's. Mr. Planche's Vampire takes the audience into his confidence, and informs them that he is a Vampire, and he doesn't desire to conceal his character. [...] Mr. Boucicault's Vampire is a sneaking, disagreeable, and rather underhanded individual, who doesn't hesitate to do a little forgery if it can be made conducive to his purpose.[71]

Here again, the critic failed to mention Boucicault's *The Vampire*, but seemed quite happy to perceive forgery as a greater sin than drinking the blood of innocent victims.[72]

By contrast, the London *Examiner* mentioned Boucicault's earlier play when critiquing *The Phantom*, to the extent that the critic quoted from Henry Morley's 1852 review. New text also appeared:

> The condemnation of the play on the first night was absolute. There were hisses during the progress of the second act. There was a preponderance of hissing, even when the curtain was raised in honor of all the actors. [...] Let us distinctly add that the play did not simply fail because the public cannot stomach a corpse hero. It is bad of its bad kind.[73]

Writing as if a twenty-first-century horror fan, the critic also condemned Boucicault's imprecise terminology: 'A solid perambulatory corpse is *not* a phantom'.[74]

The London *Era*'s critic might well have read the *Examiner* prior to writing his own review, as he also condemned the term 'Phantom' as a 'misnomer'.[75] He also observed:

> At the fall of the curtain last Monday, it would be difficult to say whether the hisses or the applause was in majority. The disapprobation, however, was levelled only at the piece—not the acting or accompaniments. Mr. Boucicault's portraiture of the half-demon, half-mortal villain, Ruthven, though deficient in voice and appearance in that romantic fascination we attach to such a character was, nevertheless, well-conceived and impressively given.
>
> [...] The whole of the piece, from beginning to end, is a mistake, an error throughout, the first and most impressive mistake being the total extinction of every trait of nationality in the story. [...] Why has he given us a once splendid *Italian Palace* in ruins, for the dilapidated walls and gloomy cells of a *Celtic Castle*?[76]

Presumably Celtic castles struck this critic as too commonplace, too familiar, in the United Kingdom, as opposed to the 'exotic' Italian settings on which gothic novelists Matthew Gregory Lewis, Ann Radcliffe and Horace Walpole had relied.

Other reviews were even harsher. A critic for the *Wells Journal* wrote, 'if any of my readers, on coming up to London, feel inclined to go and see *The Phantom*, I can only say—don't'.[77] *The Dial* explained that it was 'one of those pieces that are all the more revolting the better they are acted'.[78] And the *Morning Advertiser* brutally proclaimed, 'we cannot recollect any metropolitan theatre enjoying the high position of the Adelphi producing a drama of a more objectionable character'.[79]

By 1 June 1862, *The Phantom* ended its run at the Adelphi.[80] In July 1862, the play opened at London's St James's Theatre. The *Examiner* reported that its run lasted only one week, even though it had allegedly been 'applauded by the audience and favourably dealt with by the newspapers'.[81]

CONCLUSION

In this volume, the 1852 version of *The Vampire* and the 1873 version of *The Phantom* are presented together in one scholarly edition. Scholars and general readers can now experience Boucicault's controversial and innovative *The Vampire* for the first time, while discovering new dimensions of *The Phantom*. Boucicault's mastery of stagecraft, adaptation and sensation are on full display in both plays, although readers may also discover a different aspect of the man who struggled so mightily to gain and keep the adoration of the public that he secretly despised.

As for vampire literature and entertainment, *The Vampire* and *The Phantom* helped rewrite the history and lineage of the creature. As a result of this volume, Boucicault can take his proper place in a lineage that began with Polidori and continued through Planché, Rymer and Dumas, a lineage that after Boucicault would include J. Sheridan Le Fanu, Florence Marryat and Bram Stoker. Thanks not to moonlight, but instead to carefully preserved archival materials, Boucicault's vampires live again.

NOTES

1. 'Boucicault', *Morning Republican* (Little Rock, AR), 27 January 1873, p. 1.
2. For biographies, see Richard Fawkes, *Dion Boucicault* (London: Quartet Books, 1979); David Krause, *The Dolmen Boucicault* (Dublin: Dolmen Press, 1964); Julius H. Tolson, 'Dion Boucicault' (unpublished PhD thesis, University of Pennsylvania, 1951); Lynn Earl Orr, 'Dion Boucicault and the Nineteenth Century Theatre: A Biography' (unpublished PhD thesis, Louisiana State University, 1953).
3. See Fawkes, pp. 7–9, pp. 32–40; Krause, pp. 13–16; Tolson, pp. 13–30; Orr, pp. 17–34.
4. Deirdre McFeely, *Dion Boucicault: Irish Identity on Stage* (Cambridge: Cambridge University Press, 2012), p. 4.
5. Fawkes, pp. 65–69; Krause, p. 22; Orr, pp. 40–42.
6. Fawkes, pp. 71–77; Orr, pp. 50–53; Tolson, pp. 93–100.
7. Roxana Stuart, *Stage Blood* (Bowling Green, KY: Bowling Green State University Popular Press, 1994), p. 148.
8. Gerald Bordman and Thomas S. Hischak, eds, *The Oxford Companion to American Theatre*, 3rd edn (Oxford: Oxford University Press, 2004), p. 88.
9. Fawkes, p. 121; Orr, pp. 271–77.

10. Quoted in Fawkes, p. 242.
11. Dion Boucicault, *The Phantom: A Drama, in Two Acts* (New York: French, 1856).
12. In 1885, Boucicault married Louise Thorndyke, who was forty-three years his junior. When he died in 1890, Louise inherited a large trunk of Boucicault's prompt books and playscripts, as well as unfinished and unpublished manuscripts. Louise sold the collection in the early 1930s to novelist Fitzhugh Green, whose widow sold it in 1956 to Jack Clay, later a faculty member at the University of South Florida. See Christopher Calthrop, 'The Dion Boucicault Theatre Collection', *Ex Libris: Journal of the USF Library Associates*, 2.4 (Spring 1979), 1.
13. Agnes Robertson, 'In the Days of My Youth', *M.A.P.*, 1 July 1899, p. 636.
14. Stuart, p. 136. *Le Vampire* was first staged in Paris on 20 December 1851.
15. Sharon Gallagher, *The Irish Vampire* (Jefferson, NC: McFarland & Co., 2017), pp. 84–85; Stuart, p. 145.
16. Stuart, pp. 145 and 152.
17. Fawkes, p. 74; Stuart, p. 154.
18. Stuart, p. 154.
19. Ibid., p. 206.
20. Ibid., p. 154.
21. Gallagher, p. 42.
22. Advertisement, *The Guardian* (London), 6 March 1852, p. 6.
23. Advertisement, *Manchester Weekly Times and Examiner*, 10 March 1852, p. 4.
24. Advertisement, *Morning Post* (London), 24 April 1852, p. 8; Advertisement, *The Times* (London), 6 May 1852, p. 13.
25. Townsend Walsh, *The Career of Dion Boucicault* (New York: The Dunlap Society, 1915), p. 65.
26. Boucicault used the stage name 'Lee Moreton' for three years beginning in 1837.
27. 'Princess's Theatre', *Morning Chronicle* (London), 15 June 1852, p. 7.
28. 'Princess's Theatre: *The Vampire*', *Morning Post*, 17 June 1852, p. 5.
29. Based in London, Minerva Press published numerous gothic and 'horrid' novels from the 1780s to the 1820s, as well as other popular fare. It was the most prolific publisher of new fiction during the Romantic era.
30. 'Princess's', *Reynolds's Newspaper* (London), 20 June 1852, p. 9.
31. 'Princess's Theatre', *The Observer* (London), 20 June 1852, p. 7.
32. 'Princess's Theatre', *The Times* (London), 16 June 1852, p. 6.
33. Ibid.
34. Morley included this review in his book *The Journal of a London Playgoer from 1851 to 1856* (London: Routledge & Sons, 1891).
35. Henry Morley, 'The New Spectral Melodrama', *The Examiner* (London), 19 June 1852, p. 6.
36. 'Theatricals, Etc.', *Lloyd's Weekly Newspaper* (London), 20 June 1852, p. 11.
37. 'Music and the Drama', *Salisbury and Winchester Journal and General Advertiser of Wilts, Hants, Dorset, and Somerset*, 19 June 1852, p. 4.
38. Fawkes, p. 74.
39. 'The Drama, Music, &c.', *Reynolds's Newspaper*, 18 July 1852, p. 9.
40. 'Boucicault', *Little Rock Daily Republican*, 27 January 1873, p. 1.
41. While *The Vampire* may have been a failure, it had a lasting legacy, with Robert Reece lampooning the play in his *The Vampire: An Original Burlesque* (1872) and Gilbert and Sullivan satirizing it in *Ruddygore* (1887). Reece took aim at Boucicault's reputation for adapting some of his plots from French dramas by mak-

NOTES

ing his 'vampire' an Irish author of lowly literature who tried to steal plots from women. Reece subtitled his burlesque *A Bit of Moonshine in Three Rays*. Similarly, Gilbert and Sullivan probably made Boucicault's *The Vampire* the target of their satire, as demonstrated by their reuse of portraits coming to life. *Ruddygore* also referenced Boucicault's *The Phantom*, suggesting Gilbert and Sullivan had seen— or were familiar with—both the 1852 *Vampire* and the 1862 *Phantom*. See Stuart, pp. 164–75.

42. The time period is inconsistent in *The Phantom*, as Act II mentions the Battle of Blenheim in Germany (1704) while also utilizing a watermark of 1750 to prove a document's forgery. Act I is likely set between 1650 and 1655 and Act II between 1750 and 1755, although it appears Boucicault wavered between a 50- and 100-year gap between the vampire's murders.
43. Stuart, p. 148.
44. See *Chicago Evening Post*, 25 January 1873, p. 1.
45. See *Chicago Daily Tribune*, 26 January 1873, p. 5.
46. Advertisement, *Boston Post*, 15 September 1854, 3.
47. 'The Phantom', *Daily Pennsylvanian* (Philadelphia), 12 May 1856, p. 4.
48. 'The Theatres', *Sunday Dispatch* (Philadelphia), 18 May 1856, p. 2.
49. Ibid.
50. 'Amusements', *New York Times*, 1 July 1854, p. 4.
51. 'Wallack's Theatre–Summer Season', *New York Herald*, 2 July 1856, 4.
52. 'The World of New York', *Putnam's Monthly Magazine of American Literature, Science, and Art* (New York), 8 (September 1856), 333.
53. 'Drama', *The Albion, a Journal of News, Politics, and Literature* (New York), 19 July 1856, p. 343.
54. Advertisement, *Louisville Democrat*, 19 April 1857, p. 5.
55. Advertisement, *Washington Union* (Washington, DC), 1 January 1859, p. 3.
56. 'Boucicault in Washington', *Evening Star* (Washington, DC), 20 September 1890, p. 7. The viewer recalled the play having been produced in 1861, but he seems to have been in error, as period advertisements indicate the year was 1859.
57. Ibid.`
58. 'Barnum's Museum', *New York Dispatch*, 18 January 1863, p. 7.
59. 'Amusements', *New York Clipper*, 28 March 1863, p. 398.
60. 'Music Halls', *New York Clipper*, 24 November 1866, p. 263.
61. 'Amusement Feuilleton', *Chicago Times*, 2 February 1873, p. 5.
62. 'Amusements', *Chicago Evening Mail*, 28 January 1873, p. 4.
63. 'Amusements', *Chicago Tribune*, 28 January 1873, p. 5.
64. 'Amusements', *Inter Ocean* (Chicago), 28 January 1873, p. 4.
65. 'Amusements', *Chicago Evening Post*, 29 January 1873, p. 4.
66. 'Our London Correspondent', *Wells Journal* (Somerset), 26 April 1862, p. 3.
67. 'The Drama', *The Atlas* (London), 24 May 1862, p. 5.
68. 'Easter Amusements', *The Atlas*, 26 April 1862, p. 2.
69. 'Adelphi Theatre', *The Observer*, 27 April 1862, p. 3.
70. Ibid.
71. 'Adelphi', *The Standard*, 22 April 1862, p. 2.
72. Another critic called *The Phantom* a 'reconstruction' of Planché's play—see 'Amusements', *Illustrated Weekly News* (London), 26 April 1862, p. 458.
73. 'New Adelphi', *The Examiner*, 26 April 1862, p. 9.

74. On 26 April 1862, the *Illustrated Times* (London) wrote: 'What used to be *The Vampire* at the Princess is now *The Phantom* at the Adelphi' (p. 263). That same day, *The Press* (London) observed that '[*The Phantom*]'s interest was found wanting some years ago when it was brought out at the Princess's under the title of *The Vampire*' (p. 404).
75. 'Adelphi', *The Era* (London), 27 April 1862, p. 11.
76. Ibid.
77. 'Our London Correspondent', p. 3.
78. 'The Drama', *The Dial* (London), 26 April 1862, p. 4.
79. 'The New Adelphi Theatre', *Morning Advertiser* (London), 22 April 1862, p. 3.
80. 'The Theatres, &c.', *The Era*, 1 June 1862, p. 10.
81. 'St James's Theatre', *The Examiner*, 19 July 1862, p. 7.

SELECT BIBLIOGRAPHY

Manuscript Collections and Primary Sources

Boucicault, Dion, *The Phantom: A Drama, in Two Acts* (New York: Samuel French, 1856).

Dion Boucicault Theatre Collection, University of South Florida Libraries, Tampa Special Collections.

New York Public Library for the Performing Arts, Billy Rose Theatre Division, NCOF [Vampire].

Plays Submitted to the Lord Chamberlain, British Library Add. MS. 52932 (Q), 'The Vampire, a Phantasm Related in Three Dramas'.

Secondary Criticism

Bordman, Gerald, and Thomas S. Hischak (eds), *Oxford Companion to American Theatre,* 3rd edn (Oxford: Oxford University Press, 2004).

Calthrop, Christopher, 'The Dion Boucicault Theatre Collection', *Ex Libris, Journal of the USF Library Associates,* 2.4 (Spring 1979), 1 and 19.

Davis, J. C. *Oliver Cromwell* (London: Arnold, 2001).

Fawkes, Richard, *Dion Boucicault* (London: Quartet Books, 1979).

Gallagher, Sharon, *The Irish Vampire* (Jefferson, NC: McFarland & Co., 2017).

Krause, David, *The Dolmen Boucicault* (Dublin: The Dolmen Press, 1964).

McFeely, Deirdre, *Dion Boucicault: Irish Identity on Stage* (Cambridge: Cambridge University Press, 2012).

Morley, Henry, *The Journal of a London Playgoer from 1851 to 1856* (London: Routledge & Sons, 1891).

Orr, Lynn Earl, 'Dion Boucicault and the Nineteenth Century Theatre: A Biography' (unpublished PhD thesis, Louisiana State University, 1953).

Stuart, Roxana, *Stage Blood* (Bowling Green, KY: Bowling Green State University Popular Press, 1994).

Tolson, Julius H., 'Dion Boucicault' (unpublished PhD thesis, University of Pennsylvania, 1951).

Walsh, Townsend, *The Career of Dion Boucicault* (New York: The Dunlap Society, 1935).

Note on the Texts

THE VAMPIRE

ION BOUCICAULT'S *THE VAMPIRE* EXISTS in three unpublished sources. The first is a seventy-nine-page holograph manuscript in Boucicault's hand (hereafter, MS-V), written in April 1852.[1] MS-V is nearly complete, with only the final scene of Act III missing. The second source is a sixty-three-page handwritten script submitted to the Lord Chamberlain's Office (hereafter, LC-V), licensed on 25 May 1852 for presentation at the Royal Princess's Theatre in London.[2] The third is a handwritten prompt book (hereafter, PB-V) prepared for James Wallack of New York by Boucicault's prompter, T. H. Edmonds, in 1852.[3] While transcription errors are common in this prompt book, it is invaluable for its list of properties, scenery and stage directions. The fact that the resulting play at Wallack's Theatre was *The Phantom* and not *The Vampire* might indicate that Wallack agreed with Boucicault that American audiences were not be ready for the spectacle and literary contrivances of *The Vampire*.

LC-V and MS-V represent the foundation of the play, although they differ in many respects. MS-V includes valuable stage directions that are excluded from LC-V, and the latter also contains numerous spelling and transcription errors. Hence, MS-V is the copy text used for this edition, with significant alterations or emendations chronicled in the Emendation List (pp. 97–100). While set diagrams and blocking notes are prevalent in PB-V, they are minimal in LC-V and MS-V, and thus are present in this edition only to provide relevant contextual detail.

Boucicault's *The Vampire* has never been published in any form, and the 1856 Samuel French version of *The Phantom* was issued as 'Dick's Standard Plays No. 697' in 1885, but only differs from the French version in the dating of Act II to the mid-nineteenth century. Otherwise, the play has not been published in any altered form since.

THE PHANTOM

The text of *The Phantom* included in the present volume emerged from research into four unpublished sources, all of which are archived in the Dion Boucicault Theatre Collection at the University of South Florida. The first is a 133-page holograph prompt book in two parts (MS-P), alternating between Boucicault's hand and an unknown copyist, and bearing a watermark dated 1852. It is heavily annotated with corrections and stage directions by Boucicault. The first act is nearly identical to the version published by Samuel French in 1856. Boucicault made significant changes to Act II, however; these amendments appear in two manuscripts also bearing the same 1852 watermark. The first (HD-P), is an incomplete fourteen-page holograph draft in Boucicault's hand, and the other is a forty-nine-page handwritten rehearsal copy (RC-P), which is heavily prompted. These three manuscripts form the core of the Samuel French 1856 edition. Boucicault excised all references to the English Civil War found in HD-P for the French edition, although he did revive these references to the conflict in the 1873 version printed here. Boucicault also removed a case of mistaken identity between the lovers Stump and Jenny from HD-P, which did not appear in any subsequent version of the play. Otherwise, the handwritten versions of *The Phantom* from 1852 were nearly identical to French's published version. The 1873 text in this edition represents a more pared-down drama, with a focus on characterization and spectacle rather than comic relief and mild horror.

The present edition uses as its copy text a complete, 113-page handwritten prompt book in a copyist's hand (hereafter, PB-P), which contains numerous emendations by Boucicault. This manuscript is undated, although all evidence points to it being a revision of the 1852 text, produced for a short one-week run at McVicker's Theatre in Chicago beginning 27 January 1873.[4] The dialogue in PB-P varies greatly from the Samuel French version of *The Phantom*, and indicates both the personal preferences of Boucicault and the perceived desires of a more modern audience.

Finally, although not utilized in this edition, a handwritten rewrite of the play from 1855 moves the action from Wales to Scotland and alters character names and actions. This was the version of *The Phantom* produced in London in 1862, although the archived manuscript is unfortunately incomplete. Boucicault changed the name of the vampire to 'Ruthven' and moved the action from Raby Castle and Snowdon in Wales to Ravenscleugh and Ben Nevis in Highlands of Scotland. The manuscript contains forty pages with incomplete versions of Acts I and II. Aside from the place names, however, the action is nearly identical to *The Phantom* (1852).

THE PRESENT EDITION

Obvious errors in spelling and punctuation have been corrected silently throughout. For example, Boucicault frequently neglected to change the name of 'Davy' to 'Watkyn' in *The Vampire*, and he occasionally left out the name of the speaker. Boucicault also tended to write out his stage directions in one long run-on sentence; these have been corrected to facilitate reading and potential staging. Excepting these general emendations, few substantive changes have been made to Boucicault's original texts. Also retained are some of Boucicault's original spellings which may strike the modern reader as archaic, i.e. 'corse' for 'corpse'; 'accurst' for 'accursed'; 'musquetoon' for 'musketoon'; and so on. Stage directions have been standardized and made consistent with each other, and the list of abbreviaitons that follows below. For more details of further changes, see the Emendation List (pp. 97–100).

ABBREVIATED STAGE DIRECTIONS

The following directions are given in both play texts, and are for reader/actor facing the audience.

C.	Centre of the Stage
C.D.	Centre Door
D.L.C.	Door Left Centre
D.R.C.	Door Right Centre
L.	Left side of the Stage
L.C.	Left Centre of the Stage
L.H.	Left Hand
L.H.C.	Enters through the Centre from the Left Hand
L.U.E.	Left Upper Entrance
L.1.E.	Left First Entrance
L.2.E.	Left Second Entrance
L.3.E.	Left Third Entrance
R.	Right side of the Stage
R.C.	Right Centre of the Stage
R.H.	Right Hand
R.H.C.	Enters through the Centre from the Right Hand
R.U.E.	Right Upper Entrance
R.1.E.	Right First Entrance
R.2.E.	Right Second Entrance
R.3.E.	Right Third Entrance
U.E.	Upper Entrance

NOTES

1. Holograph manuscript of *The Vampire: A Phantasm, Related in Three Dramas* (MS-V), April 1852, Box 2, Folder 8, in Dion Boucicault Theatre Collection, MS-1963-01, USF Libraries Special Collections.
2. Original copy in the British Library, Add. Ms. 52932 (Q).
3. New York Public Library for the Performing Arts, Billy Rose Theatre Division, NCOF [*Vampire*].
4. See *Chicago Evening Post*, 25 January 1873, p. 1.

Artwork of Boucicault's *The Phantom*,
Frank Leslie's Illustrated Newspaper, 26 July 1856

The Vampire, a Phantasm[1] in Three Dramas

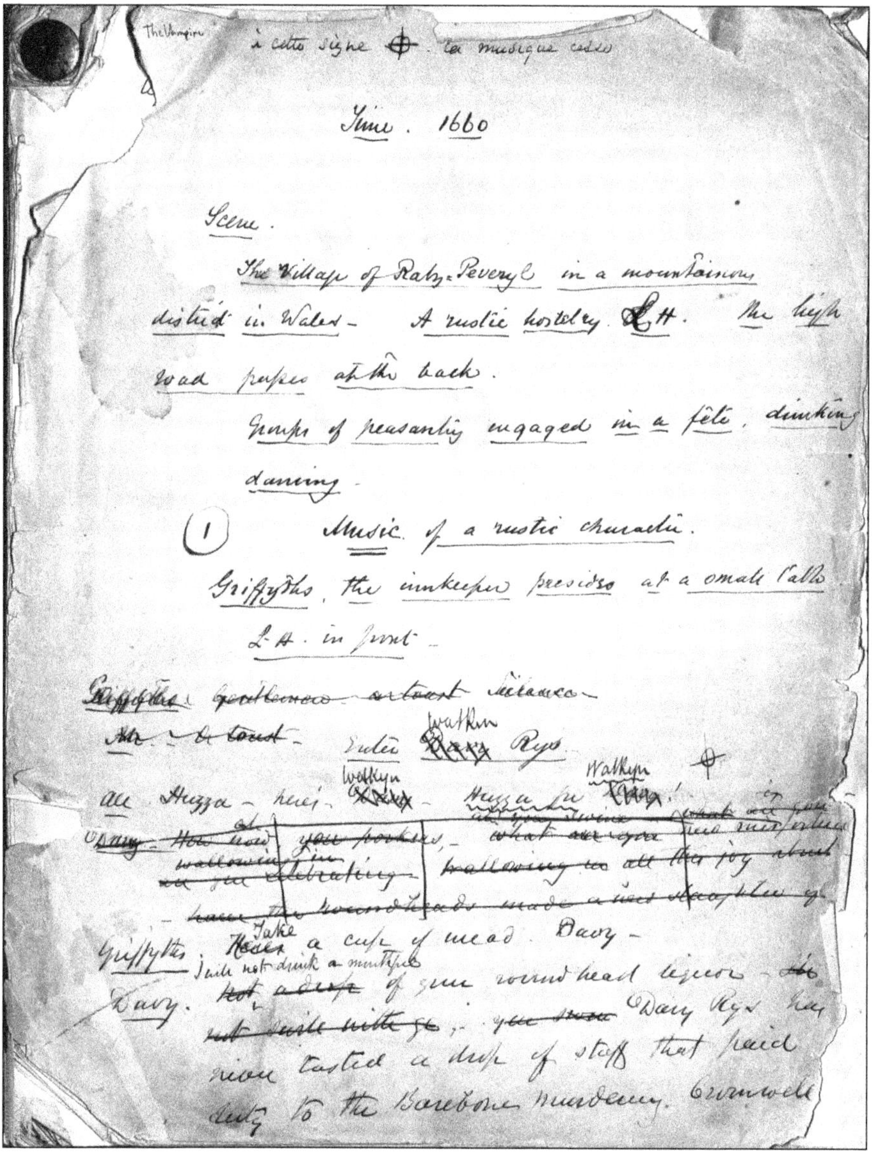

Figure 1. First page of Boucicault's handwritten manuscript of *The Vampire* (MS-V). Courtesy University of South Florida Libraries Special Collections, Dion Boucicault Theatre Collection.

Characters in the First Drama

Sir Alan Raby
Lord Arthur Clavering
Sir Guy Musgrave
Foulke Nevil of Greystock
Ralph ap Gwynne
Lady Ellen Clavering
Maud Nevil of Greystock
Watkyn Rhys
Griffiths
Lucy Peveryl
Villagers
Male and female servants
Waiter

The First Drama—Raby Castle

SCENE ONE

Time: 1660. Scene: The Village of Raby Peveryl[1] *in a mountainous district in Wales—a rustic hostelry R.H. The high road passes at the back. Groups of peasantry engaged in a fete,*[2] *drinking and dancing. Music of a rustic character.* GRIFFITHS, *the innkeeper, presides at a small table L.H. in front. Enter* WATKYN RHYS *R.H.*

ALL.   Huzza! Here's Watkyn. Huzza for Watkyn!

GRIF.   Take a cup of mead,[3] Watkyn.

WAT.   I will not drink a mouthful of your roundhead[4] liquor. Watkyn Rhys has never tasted a drop of stuff that paid duty to the barbarous, murdering Cromwell.[5] I live in the peaks of Snowdon[6]—there I brew my own liquor. The roebuck[7] and the goat afford me food and clothing, and I can drink aloud—confusion to the Puritan[8] crew that laid the walls of Raby low.

GRIF.   Nonsense. The land now is a waste land. We pay no rent—the lords of Raby were good landlords; but there's something better than a good landlord, and that's no landlord at all.

WAT.   Well, what new misfortune are you celebrating with all this joy? I suppose the canting Cromwell has made himself king of England—may the fiend[9] preserve him.

GRIF.   Amen—he is dead![10]

WAT.   Dead—Cromwell dead!

ALL.   Ay.

WAT.   Give me the cup of mead.

GRIF.   Stay—let me read you the proclamation. Here it is.

WAT.   A proclamation—let me see. Signed—Charles! King Charles restored![11] England, I forgive you. (*all laugh*) Let me read. No, stop! Hark you all—(*he takes off his hat*) here's to the memory of Charles the First.[12] (*he drinks, all the peasants take off their hats; he flings the cup over his head*) God save King Charles the Second.

ALL.   Huzzah! Huzzah!

He reads proclamation aside—kisses the signature with the greatest demonstration of joy. Sits R.H. Enter LUCY PEVERYL *L.H.*

GRIF.   A lady. (*bows; all doff their caps*)

LUCY.   Good people, tell me—is not this the village of Raby?

GRIF.   Ay, please your ladyship.

LUCY.   I have ridden far to reach this place before sunset. Pray give my jennet food and housing.

GRIF.   Lead in the lady's horse there. (*exeunt peasants*) Is your ladyship alone?

LUCY.   I had the protection of an escort as far as Tremadoc.[13] A party of noble cavaliers[14] and ladies riding to their newly recovered estates.[15]

GRIF.   Our exiled nobles are glad to see their homes and lands once more. Many such parties have passed my inn, but I have only room to shelter the footsore traveller who can relish our Welsh fare and homely mead. Will your ladyship take a cup after your fatigue?

LUCY.   I thank you, no. My journey is not ended. I must proceed afoot.

GRIF.   Afoot!

LUCY.   Can you not find me some honest guide who can conduct me to the ruins of Raby Castle?

GRIF.   To the ruins of Raby, and tonight?

LUCY.   Is it not possible to reach the spot by nightfall?

GRIF.   (*to the peasants*) You hear the lady asks a guide to Raby Castle. (*the crowd recoil in terror at the mention of Raby*)

WAT.   (*looking up*) Who seeks the ruins at such an hour? (*rises*) What can you want in such a place? Who are you?

LUCY. I am one to whom you would owe more courtesy and obedience, did a lord of Raby live. My name is Lucy Peveryl. (*movement of surprise and pleasure among the peasantry*)

WAT. A Peveryl! (*runs to her and kisses her hand*) There's not a letter in the name we do not love. Speak, what shall we do to serve you?

LUCY. I will trust you. Listen. The life of one dear, most dear to me is in danger. He flies from death. Today he crosses the Welsh frontier[16] on his road to Milford.[17] He has written to me here to tell me that on this night the 15th of August he will seek shelter and a moment's rest in the ruins of Raby Castle.

GRIF. Stay—a fair young man, is he not? With a slight scar upon his chin?

LUCY. The same.

GRIF. He was here an hour ago. (*to a peasant girl*) Here, Mercy Gaveston, you watched him as he went. He spoke with you.

GIRL. He asked me whereabouts the old castle was. I told him and he wandered there away.

LUCY. 'Twas he! 'Twas he! He awaits me. Oh, I will reward you nobly— guide me thither.

WAT. Not I. Not for King Charles' crown.

GRIF. The place is accurst.

WAT. The threshold is red with the blood of Ralph and Owen Raby, shed by their own brother's hand. It has never dried up—the earth would not drink it.

LUCY. I know the fearful tragedy in which was extinguished our noble race.

WAT. But you do not know the welcome which awaits those who seek the shelter of these ruins?

LUCY. (*smiling*) Indeed!

WAT. The same that Alan Raby gave his brothers—death!

LUCY. Death—it is then the resort of robbers?

WAT.   No robbers at all. No human being ever sets foot there—but those fools who never return, and their doom is dealt out by no mortal hand.

LUCY.   Oh, you foolish people. I see that you believe the place is haunted—you have seen goblins,[18] eh?

WAT.   No I haven't. But I have heard.

ALL.   Ay.

WAT.   On the anniversary of the deed, the old clock in the ruined tower chimes the hour of midnight; yet no hand for fifteen years has touched the dial. Its works are gone; its bell is tongueless; yet from the peaks of Snowdon I have heard it toll.

LUCY.   No goblin legend shall hinder me—will you accompany me?

WAT.   No.

LUCY.   Then I will go alone.

WAT.   No, neighbours, don't let her stir.

ALL.   Ay! Ay!

They close up and oppose her going. Sunset breaks over the scene. Enter a travelling party consisting of LORD ARTHUR CLAVERING, NEVIL *of* GREYSTOCK, RALPH ap GWYNNE,[19] SIR GUY MUSGRAVE, LADY ELLEN, MAUD NEVIL, *servants and retainers.*

ARTH.   Hail to Raby Peveryl. Bless your merry Welsh faces, and long live every peak of ill-tempered old Snowdon. Ho! Where's the innkeeper? Where's old Griffiths?

GRIF.   Bless me! Why sure 'tis the young Lord Arthur Clavering. (*movement of joy amongst peasantry*)

ARTH.   Ay, as gay as ever in spite of my ten years of exile. But give our horses food; we will but refresh and then on to Llanberis.[20]

GRIF.   The mountain road is dangerous, my Lord, and there's a frown on Snowdon that means mischief to the night.

ELLEN.   Why should we not pass the night in this village?

GRIF. Alas, lady, you see my poor roof will not shelter a quarter of your party.

One of the servants R.H. who has been flirting with one of the peasant girls endeavours to snatch a kiss. A peasant lad interposes and takes her away up bridge L.U.E.

MAUD. Courage, then, let us push on and try this mountain road.

NEVIL. I am most anxious to reach my estate tonight if possible.

WAT. Then you must be long in the reach, Master Nevil, for no mortal creature will pass the Mill gap[21] when Snowdon shakes her cloudy head.

MUS. (*looking at* WATKYN) What species of quadruped is this?

ARTH. Why Watkyn Rhys, my old friend. (*shaking his hand*) Why, ha! ha! What a strange figure you are, Watkyn—have the rascally roundheads brought you to this?

WAT. Bless your lordship; many's the hour we've watched an old trout together, and climbed the mountain after a roebuck.

ARTH. When I was on a visit to my cousins Ralph and Owen Raby—you remember, Nevil, the dreadful history of their death?

NEV: Noble fellows. I remember well they fought beside me at Naseby.[22]

MUS. I was not in time for the battle, but I joined in the retreat. (MAUD *laughs at him, retires up, joins* ELLEN *and they promenade at back*)

RALPH. Their regiment protected the King's flight, repulsing a charge of Ireton's dragoons.[23]

ARTH. That charge was led by their own brother. Alan Raby, the youngest of the family, was destined to the Church, he espoused the cause of Cromwell and became one of the most furious of his fanatic followers. 'Twas he who pursued the shattered regiment of his brothers when they retreated to Raby Castle. The place was carried by assault, and it is said that the puritan looked on while his myrmidons[24] butchered his brothers on their own threshold.

MUS. This fellow did not deserve to die like a gentleman.

ARTH. Ay, and scarcely had he possessed himself of his new inheritance when a royalist division swept across this country. The castle was surprised, and the murderer was hurled from a turret window down the precipice on the brink of which the castle stands.

NEV. Surely there is enough of the place standing to afford us shelter for the night. What say you, gentlemen—shall we to Raby?

ALL THE PARTY. Ay! To Raby!

LUCY. (*who has been seated and lost in abstraction, rises at the word*) To Raby!

MAUD. Agreed. Eh, Sir Guy, this history will give a thrilling interest to the spot.

MUS. So it will—but I don't like the idea.

MAUD. We will pass a night of romance. Now if it were only haunted, how delightful that would be.

MUS. Charming indeed. (*aside*) It would be like sleeping in a stable full of nightmares.

LUCY. (*advancing*) My lord, pardon me, I know you by name for a noble gentleman. My name is Lucy Peveryl—I claim your aid.

ARTH. A fairer name never graced so fair a lady. Command me.

LUCY. Read, read. (*gives him a letter; he looks at the signature*)

ARTH. Roland Peveryl! My schoolfellow. My friend until this civil strife separated us, but not our hearts.

LUCY. See his life is forfeit. He flies from death.

ARTH. (*reading*) Tonight he will rest a while in the ruins of Raby.

LUCY. There we meet, and it may be for the last time. He is an outlaw—a rebel.

ARTH. Ay, but as gallant and noble a fellow as ever drew bright steel.

LUCY. Oh, sir, thanks for that soft word when all heap execration on him. (*takes* ARTHUR's *hand*)

ARTH. You love him?

LUCY. I do, I do! And that I may see him once more, that I may send him from his native land with my plighted troth and with hope in his heart. I have braved the wrath of my haughty brother and the dangers of the road. I am here—permit me to join your party.

A distant storm. ARTHUR *introduces* LUCY *to* ELLEN *and* MAUD NEVIL.

NEV. Hark! The storm comes down the mountain.

WAT. My lord, Lord Arthur, you will not dare to pass the night in Raby.

ARTH. Why not?

WAT. You forget that this day, the 15th of August, is the anniversary of the deed of blood.

ARTH. Why should that circumstance spoil my night's rest?

WAT. Why? I will tell you why. (*all move forward listening*) Because you think to find an empty house, but you will find a host you little think to meet. Because others besides yourselves would not be warned, but have sought shelter there.

ARTH. What did they behold?

WAT. They never lived to tell.

ALL. How?

WAT. When we searched the ruins for them by daylight, we found them—dead.

ARTH. Dead!

WAT. With a deep wound here in the heart.

ARTH. Ha! ha! Bravo, friend Watkyn. You hear, Ellen? Will you dare the mysteries of this enchanted castle? Decide—the storm comes on apace. (*the peasantry gradually have returned as if to avoid the storm*)

LUCY. Oh, I beseech you!

MAUD. Forward, then. Come, Sir Guy.

Mus. As your ladyship observes—forward. (*aside*) I don't like this idea at all.

Arth. Ho! Within there—bring after us wine, food and wherewithal to pass a jovial night.

The servants hurry across to precede the party.

(*to* Lucy) Now, fair lady, forward to Raby.

All. To Raby!

Wat. My lord, lord Arthur!

A flash of lightning and a deafening roll of thunder. The stage has become dark. The party go off lighted by the servants who precede and follow them with packages. Watkyn *follows entreating with gestures of despair.*

SCENE TWO

The ruins of Raby Castle. A hall and a vaulted opening L.C. leads to a ruined staircase. A window with a broken balcony R.H. in flat is supposed to overhang a precipice. Without are seen crags and rocks. In the distance is seen the clock tower. Night. A storm. Enter Arthur *with a torch by the ruined staircase.*

Arth. So, this chamber will serve us well. Here is at least a roof. Ho, Nevil, Gwynne!

Nev. (*from beneath*) Hillo!

Arth. (*from the window, holding out his torch*) Here in the turret chamber—mount the ruined stair. (*lights are seen to flash from the stair*)

Enter Musgrave *from R.H. door.*

Mus. Where the devil am I? I don't like this place at all. (Arthur *advances*) I just mistook a window for a door, and was feeling my way out at a precipice a thousand feet deep. I don't like this place, but where have they all got to? Hillo!

Arth. Eh! (*slaps* Musgrave *on the shoulder; he starts,* Arthur *laughs*)

The whole party now have mounted the stair and advance; the servants dress a table R.H.

Well, where have you all been?

ELLEN.   I have been with Nevil to explore the vaults and cloisters.

MAUD.   I mounted to the top of a strange square tower and beheld the vagaries of the storm amongst the mountain crags. It was sublime, was it not Sir Guy?

MUS.   Poetical indeed. But I never did like poetry.

MAUD.   I sent him to find you, but I suppose you lost yourself.

MUS.   Yes, and I would have given a large reward to anybody who could have found me in any place but this. I don't like the idea of this spot at all. I think I said so before.

RALPH.   Come to supper, Lady Ellen, allow me.

ARTH.   Miss Peveryl. (*offers his hand to her*)

LUCY.   No, oh, no. I could not join your party. Roland—Roland is not here.

ELLEN.   He has found some other shelter during the storm.

ARTH.   He will surely join us ere long.

LUCY.   Pardon me—a presentiment of evil weighs upon my heart. Hark! How the storm rages. The mountain road is full of perils.

ARTH.   I will wave a torch from yonder balcony; if he be within signal, it will guide him hither. (ARTHUR *and* LUCY *go out on the ruined balcony*)

MAUD.   Come, Sir Guy, look cheerful. Your nose is lengthening visibly and paling at the tip—besides your wig is getting out of curl.[25]

MUS.   Yes. I caught an abominable bat[26] in it. I dare say the creature mistook it for a tree, and I could not get him over the idea.

ARTH.   (*waving the torch*) Roland!

LUCY.   Roland! Roland! (*thunder*)

ELLEN. Come, pledge[27] me, Master Nevil. Fill Master Gwynne.

MAUD. Now, Sir Guy, now. I am waiting for a glass of burgundy[28]—will you join me?

MUS. I like that idea greatly. (*he fills glasses, drinks and then fills a tumbler which he quaffs at a draught*)

ARTH. (*waves his torch*) Roland!

LUCY. Roland! Roland!

MUS. (*aside*) I must get drunk in self-defense. (ARTHUR *and* LUCY *advance*)

MAUD. Come, I must persuade you, Miss Peveryl, be seated. Sit here, Arthur.

ARTH. (*to* LADY ELLEN'*s waiting woman*) Retire with these fellows. Prepare yonder room (*points R.*) for Miss Peveryl. Those above for Miss Nevil and my sister. Three of you gentlemen will find housing in the hall below. You, Musgrave, being tender, shall have the clock tower. The chamber that once held the machinery is empty—a few rusty wheels excepted.

MUS. I had rather be near the ladies.

ARTH. That is my post. I will watch here tonight. (*to servants*) There should be in yonder corner a panel which conceals a secret stair by which the rooms above may be approached. (*the servants search for the panel and open it, showing a staircase in the wall*) Nevil, until my hour of sentry begin, take a musquetoon[29] and mount my guard for me while I sup. (NEVIL *rises and stands in the vaulted entry with a musquetoon, having previously lighted a match*)

NEVIL. I say, Clavering, does not this place and this night remind you of our adventure in Holstein?[30]

ARTH. (*drinking*) Ay, by St. George,[31] 'tis singularly like.

RALPH. What was it?

MUS. Ay, (*drinks*) what was it?

ARTH. Fill, and I will tell you.

LUCY. (*aside*) Oh, what weight of dread is this about my heart.

ARTH. We were campaigning in Northern Germany when Nevil there and I were billeted in a fine castle—as we thought. But when we were guided to our destination, we found just such a place as this—a perfect ruin. However, the night was stormy and we were glad of any shelter. The next morning we found that our appearance excited the greatest wonder in the village, and on inquiry in appeared that the castle was reputed to be haunted—just as this may be—but by a being unknown to our native legends: by a vampire!

ELLEN and MAUD. A Vampire!

LUCY. (*aside*) He comes not, he comes not. Oh Roland! Roland!

ARTH. Yes, a vampire—an absurd idea, but credited by many. They say that when a human being dies who has shed the blood of his own kindred, a father or brother, the very earth revolting from the enormity of the crime will give him no sepulture. Then the Demon[32] endows that corpse with a frightful existence, which is sustained by the blood of the living on whom this monster preys.

ELLEN. Arthur, how can you fill our minds with such thoughts.

MUS. (*aside*) I can't get drunk. I don't know why—but I can't.

MAUD. (*to* MUSGRAVE) What a horrid idea.

MUS. It is horrid, but I can't. (*drinks*)

ARTH. I give you the legend as I had it from those who believed it. (*drinks*)

MAUD. It is impossible.

LUCY. Oh, surely some calamity has befallen him.

NEVIL. Ho there! Someone mounts the ruined stair—alert!

He retreats down the stage. The gentlemen seize their swords and advance. In the vaulted opening there appears a dark figure dressed in the puritan garb.[33] The face of the figure is deadly pale. It is ALAN RABY.

ARTH. Who art thou?

ALAN. I am a stranger, benighted in the storm. I was informed a noble company had sought shelter here. I come to claim your hospitality.

ALL. A puritan!

ALAN. Ay, a puritan. One who has been your foe, but in a night like this, when the voice of heaven is loud, the wrath of man should hold its peace.

ARTH. Advance, sir, you need not teach us courtesy. (ALAN RABY *advances*) This is my sister, sir, Lady Ellen Clavering, and this Mistress Maud Nevil of Greystock, whose brother you see there with Master Gwynne. Here Miss Lucy Peveryl, and I, sir, am Arthur Clavering of Welwyn. Whom may we have the honour to entertain?

ALAN. One Gervase Rookwood, a poor gentleman who owes his presence in your noble company more to your courtesy than his own deserts.

ARTH. Sir, you are welcome.

NEVIL. (*aside to* RALPH) What a strange figure!

RALPH. Do you remark that unnatural pallor?

NEVIL. Had I a pencil here I would sketch him as he stands.

MAUD. There's Lady Ellen's sketching book.

NEVIL. Bring it here, Maud.

MAUD *brings book from table.* NEVIL *kneels and begins sketching.*

ARTH. We have not supped, sir; pray you be seated. I will join you.

Enter WATKYN RHYS.

WAT. Here I am at last.

ARTH. (*seating himself*) What, Watkyn, you have overcome your fears, then?

WAT. No. I followed you so far that I was more afraid of going back than seeking you to implore you to return with me. Do, Lord Arthur.

ARTH. Nonsense. Take our guest's cloak and sword and lay them by.

WATKYN *advances behind* ALAN RABY, *takes his cloak and sword, catches a glimpse of his face and stands horror-struck.* ALAN RABY, *who has never removed his eyes from* LUCY, *now sits near her.*

WAT. (*to* MUSGRAVE) Sir, sir, do you know this, this, gentleman? Is he of your party?

MUS. Know him. Is a rascally roundhead of my party? What d'ye take me for? If I had my will, instead of a supper I would give him a bellyful of steel and throw him from yonder turret window.

WAT. It would not be the first time he has been thrown from yonder turret window.

MUS. Eh?

WAT. (*wiping his brow with his sleeve*) No, don't heed me. No! It cannot be. My terror cheats my senses.

ARTH. Why Watkyn, you look pale. Come, drink a horn of Burgundy. (*hands him a horn of wine*)[34]

WAT. Thanks. (*drinks*)

MAUD. Now, Master Watkyn, tell us all about this place. You must know the locality.

WAT. Too well, Madam, too well.

MAUD. What room is this?

WAT. It was called the turret chamber. 'Twas here that Al—Al—(*looks at* ALAN RABY) Alan Raby passed his hours of study and seclusion.

ARTH. (*passing with a bottle to C. and filling* WATKYN's *horn again*) And perhaps in his youthful hours meditated the means of committing the horrible crime by which he possessed himself of his brothers' inheritance.

WAT. I should not wonder. (*drinks*)

LUCY. (*suddenly rises and goes to* ARTHUR. ALAN *takes her seat*) I know not what possesses me—a shapeless terror haunts me. Pardon my importunity.

ARTH. Do not fear, for see the storm abates. Roland has sought some passing shelter while it raged; he will be here assuredly. Be calm.

LUCY. (*aside*) The presence of this stranger appals me—his gaze chills my heart.

ARTH. This is the wantonness of fear. Nay, be advised, take some refreshment.

LUCY *turns to sit. Sees* ALAN *in her chair. He motions to her to sit in front of table, which* LUCY *slowly takes as if unconsciously. The storm having cleared away, through the window is dimly seen the clock tower.*

MAUD. See, Ellen, here's a scene for your pencil. See yonder lofty tower.

WAT. Ay, that is the clock tower.

MUS. My bed chamber.

WAT. At this very moment fifteen years ago, the murderous attack was going on below. The court was strewn with dead. At this very moment, two brothers stood back to back and sword in hand upon their own hearthstone. When Alan Raby sheeted in blood strode into the hall, he raised his hand and a hundred bullets stretched them dead. (*drinks*)

MUS. (*aside*) I'm glad I don't sleep in this body of the building. I should not like the idea.

WAT. When Ralph and Owen Raby fell, the turret clock struck the hour of twelve, and although its works are rusted now, and rotted all away, still as each year comes round, at the moment of the crime the empty bell chimes midnight.

MUS. Heh, what? My bedroom strikes twelve! And tonight is the anniversary. I won't sleep there, I don't like the idea.

ARTH. What say you to this massacre, Master Rookwood?

ALAN. I say, it is not for us to judge. The forfeit has been paid, here and hereafter.

WAT. I don't know that. When the royalists surprised the castle, they found the murderer in this very room. They would not soil their noble steel with felon's blood—and so they hurled him from yonder turret window.

ARTH. There is a precipice below of untold depth.

MUS. I know—1000 feet at least. I nearly measured it.

NEVIL. He was dashed to pieces.

WAT. When the castle was demolished and the troops gone, we searched the rocks below but no sign of Alan Raby's body could we find.

ALL. How?

WAT. None. They say the earth refused its shelter to the fratricide.[35] Alan Raby is dead but has not passed the grave.

ARTH. Come, gentlemen, 'tis time to seek our rest. The night is well advanced. We must be stirring early.

MUS. I will positively not sleep in that clock—suppose it should suddenly begin to go?

MAUD. I will share Ellen's chamber—you can occupy that destined for me.

MUS. Whoever heard of retiring to rest in a clock?

During this time the servants have come on, removed the supper and leave a candle burning on the table. LADY ELLEN *and* MAUD *go off with attendants at secret staircase.* NEVIL, MUSGRAVE, *and* RALPH *exeunt by ruined staircase C.* LUCY PEVERYL *goes into R.H. chamber.* ALAN RABY *at the same moment passes through a panel at back R.H.* ARTHUR *is left with* WATKYN.

ARTH. Now, Watkyn, leave me. I would pass the night alone.

WAT. But at that rate so must I!

ARTH. There is a chamber.

WAT. Alan Raby's bedroom!

ARTH. Nonsense. I am weary of this folly—leave me!

WAT. Yes, my lord. I—am going—did your lordship call?

ARTH. No. Begone.

WAT. Yes. I am. I—Lord how dark it is. I beg pardon, but you have not about you a morsel of candle?

ARTH. Away, I tell you. The moon will shortly rise, and you will have light enough.

WAT.   I am going. (*in his absence of mind he takes up the candle*) Good night. (ARTHUR *takes candle*) I beg your pardon, I'm going, good night.

ARTH.   Good night, Watkyn.

WAT.   I forgot to say good night.

ARTH.   Will you leave me.

WAT.   Yes, my lord. Don't you see, I am leaving you. (*sings*) 'Of all the birds that sing so sweet; when of an Eventide; upon the hawthorn bough they meet; to carol side by side'.[36]

WATKYN *is heard to utter a shout from the chamber.* ARTHUR *starts up.* WATKYN *rushes in, falls on knees, clutches* ARTHUR's *arm.*

ARTH.   How now?

WAT.   There! There!

ARTH.   What? Speak.

WAT.   Somebody.

ARTH.   Someone in your chamber? (WATKYN *nods*) Impossible!

WAT.   Someone on the ground, I tell you. I was searching for a soft place to lie me down. I found what seemed to be a heap of clothes. Scarce had I laid me down, when I found my pillow was a human corse.

ARTH.   If this alarm be but the creature of your brain, I will cut your coward ears off.

Takes candle and goes into chamber, loaded pistol in his hand. ARTHUR *re-enters mute and horror-struck.*

> Horror—'tis true. A murderous deed has been freshly done. There lies young Roland Peveryl, weltering in his blood, a wound deep in his heart. And there he lay while we were feasting here, while wine flowed and laughter rang—oh, horrible mockery! And she too—wretched girl, whose fears I derided, she sleeps—sleeps there while her lover lies a corse.[37] No, it must not be, she shall quit this fatal place. (*a prolonged cry heard from* LUCY) That cry—it is her voice! (*another cry for help*) Perdition! She is not alone.

The candle is extinguished. LUCY *enters from chamber; her hands clutch her neck as she reels forward.*

Lucy! Lucy!

LUCY.   Help me! Murdered! (*falls dead*)

ARTH.   Murdered! (ALAN RABY *enters from her chamber*) Ha! A form steals from her chamber.

Fires at ALAN, *who falls on table. Enter* NEVIL, MUSGRAVE, RALPH *and servants with lights.* ELLEN *and* MAUD *appear on the staircase.*

Rookwood!

ALAN.   (*raises himself from table*) What have you done? I heard a cry—a cry for help. It came from a chamber next to that in which I slept. I burst the door of communication and entered only in time to see the murderer escape. He fled by the window. I hurried hither to obtain assistance, when— (*falls*)

ARTH.   I have murdered him. (*the turret clock begins to strike twelve.* WATKYN *starts and listens at window*)

ALAN.   Ay, I die by your hand.

ARTH.   Oh, sir, forgive me. Let not your blood lie upon my soul—for I am innocent of murder. (*kneels at his feet*)

ALAN.   Stand apart. (*all retreat*) On one condition I will forgive thee—one.

ARTH.   Name it.

ALAN.   By the tenets of the religious sect whose faith I rigidly profess, the dead must be consigned into the grave with an especial ceremony.

ARTH.   I will perform it—speak.

ALAN.   When I have breathed my last let my body be conveyed amongst the peaks of Snowdon, and there exposed to the first rays of the rising moon which touch the earth.

ARTH.   It shall be done. I swear it.

ALAN.   Enough. I accept the oath. (*he dies*)

ARTHUR *buries his face in his hand. The characters form a group. Curtain descends.*

SCENE THREE

The peaks of Snowdon. All the scene has a desolate appearance. On a ledge of rock half-scene high ARTHUR CLAVERING *is discovered with the body of* ALAN RABY *in his arms. He lays down the body and then descends a winding track.*

ARTH.   I have redeemed my oath. Oh, let me hasten from this unearthly spot—this deathlike solitude. (*he descends out of sight*)

A pause. The moonlight is seen to tip the highest peaks and creep down the mountain side. It arrives at the ledge, and bathes the body of ALAN RABY *in a bright white light. Pause. The chest and various parts of the body begin to quiver. He raises his arm to his heart and revives completely, rising to his full height.*

ALAN.   (*addressing the moon*) Fountain of my life, once more thy rays restore me. Death—I do defy thee.

Music forte.[38] *Curtain descends.*

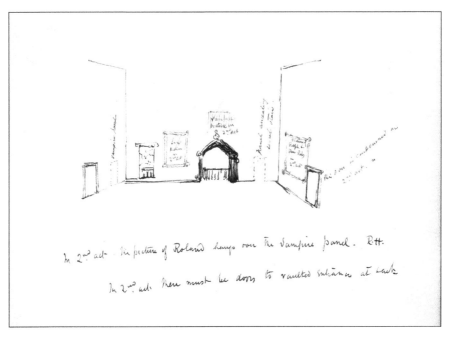

Figure 2. Boucicault's sketch of the stage design for the Second Drama in *The Vampire* (MS-V). Courtesy University of South Florida Libraries Special Collections, Dion Boucicault Theatre Collection.

Characters in the Second Drama

Sir Alan Raby
Edgar Peveril
Trevanian
Wilton Forsyth
Watty Rhys
Lady Peveril
Alice Peveril
Augusta Nevil

The Portraits:
Ralph and Owen Raby in one frame *L.H.*
Lucy Peveryl *C.*
Roland Peveryl *R.H.*

The Second Drama—Raby Hall

Time: 15th August, 1760. Scene: Raby Hall. The turret chamber represented in Act I, but now restored. The window, door, the same as before. The room is richly decorated. Over the staircase at back hangs a brilliant chandelier.[1] Around the room are hung the following portraits: in a large frame L.H. at back, RALPH *and* OWEN RABY. *R.C. of flat* LUCY PEVERYL[2] *as dressed in Act I. R.H.* ROLAND PEVERYL. *Over the vaulted entrance C. a portrait covered with a black veil. In the room a group of ladies and gentlemen dressed in the style of George III[3] are discovered engaged in a soirée.[4] A settee L.H. near which is a small gilt table on which a shaded lamp is burning. A group of young people L.H. playing at hunt the slipper.[5] An old lady and gentleman R.H. playing at ombre or piquet[6] at table.* AUGUSTA NEVIL *is seated on the settee R.H., to whom* TREVANION *and* WILTON FORSYTH *are paying devotion. The music of a minuet[7] is heard. Ladies and gentlemen are seen ascending and descending the staircase C. A general buzz of conversation and laughter. Enter* LADY PEVERYL *L.H.*

AUG.   Dear Lady Peveryl, will you take one of these men away.

LADY P.   For shame, Augusta.

AUG.   Well, Aunt, the weather is very oppressive, and I am between two roaring furnaces. I shall be fairly burnt out.

TREV.   Thus you will die the death of a wasp as you are.

FOR.   That is excruciatingly true.

AUG.   Get away, both of you. (*rising and going to* LADY PEVERYL) Dear aunt, you look pale and careworn.

LADY P.   I cannot conceal my anxiety. You know that today is Edgar's birthday.

AUG.   Do we not inaugurate the event with this (*laughter without*)—ahem, with this solemnity?

LADY P.   But I had reserved a surprise for you all, which you little dreamed of. Last week I received a letter from Florence[8] from my dear boy, in which he not only announced his immediate return—

AUG. Edgar—coming back.

LADY P. But promised to arrive here on this day.

AUG. Edgar, my handsome cousin Edgar. Trevanion, Mr. Forsyth, unhappy men, do you hear? You must return into that obscurity from which you have too rashly emerged—and you never shewed me this letter, aunt, I withdraw from you my esteem. Where is it?

LADY P. Alice has it, I believe. Ah, here she is.

Enter ALICE PEVERYL *on the arm of a gentleman. She fans herself.*

ALICE. Ah, dear Mamma, such a minuet.

AUG. Yes, yes, delightful. A young lady's last dance always is. We will take it for granted that you and your partner dipped and ducked, and bobbed and bowed and slid away like a pair of ducks just after taking to the water; but, you little traitor, never to tell me of Edgar's letter, you deserve to be sunburnt. Where is it?

ALICE. (*drawing the letter from her bosom*) Here it is.

AUG. (*takes it*) My first and only love. I have not seen him since I was nine years old, but I have a lock of his dear mud-coloured hair still. Beg pardon, aunt, but you know all boys have the same coloured hair. I suppose it saves nature trouble. Sweet Edgar. (*kisses the letter*) I wish my name was Emma. Edgar and Emma,[9] you know. Ah, dear! What an intellectual handwriting—not a word of it legible—which is the right side of it—oh, so! 'Florence. 1st July Old Style 1760'.[10] (*reads*)

LADY P. You see. He says he will arrive upon his birthday, the 15th of August.

AUG. How fondly he speaks of that gentleman—his travelling companion.

LADY P. All his letters are filled with his praises.

ALICE. Really. Edgar has drawn such a picture of this friend of his that I am half in love with him already.

LADY P. He saved my son's life, and from all I can learn of his character, he is just such a companion as I would have selected for my dear Edgar.

AUG. Not a word about me in the letter, the bear.

ALICE.   Oh, yes! You have the postscript all to yourself.

AUG.   So I have—the duck! (*reads*) 'Don't forget to invite little Augusta Nevil. She was such a droll[11] child. What a pity she was so plain; but perhaps she has outgrown it'. (LADY PEVERYL *and* ALICE *turn away laughing*) Why, Trevanion! How can you stand there? Why don't you fly out—explode—and speak. Have I outgrown it?

TREV.   You were always perfection—a Venus.[12]

FOR.   Yes, a Venus—improved by a hoop[13] and powder.[14]

ALICE.   My dear Augusta. Edgar has been studying the fine arts[15] in Italy, his eye for beauty has been educated and he will find you exquisite.

AUG.   If he does not I will go into a nunnery.

TREV. & FOR.   Oh!

AUG.   I will do so incontinently. (*a distant shout is heard*)

ALICE.   Hark! (*another shout with the cracking of a whip*)

LADY P.   'Tis he—'tis Edgar—'tis my son!

Loud shouts beneath. General movement on the stage. Several go to the window and then go to look over the staircase.

EDGAR.   (*without*) Where—where is she?

ALICE.   'Tis Edgar's voice—he is come.

The crowd divides and EDGAR PEVERYL *enters from staircase C. and advances rapidly and embraces* LADY PEVERYL *and* ALICE.

EDGAR.   My dearest mother. Bless you a thousand times.

LADY P.   My son, my darling boy!

EDGAR.   My sweet Alice. How you are changed in three years.

ALICE.   Not in my love for you, Edgar.

AUG.   He does not take the slightest notice of me.

EDGAR.   And here are all my old friends—Trevanion—Forsythe! (*shakes hands with them*) All come to welcome me.

AUG.   He does not know me. I'm so glad.

EDGAR.   (*gazing on* AUGUSTA) Why surely it cannot be.

AUG.   Yes, it is.

EDGAR.   No.

AUG.   Yes.

EDGAR.   Augusta Nevil—this pocket Venus!

AUG.   Aha! I have outgrown it. Oh, Edgar, how Italy has improved you. Oh, it has really. I'm so glad to see you. (*shaking hands heartily with him and putting her face up to him*) You may, if you like. (*he kisses her*)

EDGAR.   As wild as ever.

AUG.   Yes, wild as a hawk. Sir Harry Pointer followed me for two years, but he said I always got up out of shot. (*all laugh*)

EDGAR.   Well, you see, dear Mother, I have kept my word. But I must not take credit for what I do not deserve. Had it not been for my indefatigable companion, I had not arrived today.

LADY P.   I gave you up at last.

EDGAR.   But he seemed to know every inch of the road, and if I pleaded for a moment's rest, he would recall to me your eager, watching face. How you would read and reread my promise to be here on my birthday, the 15th of August.

LADY P.   How well he knew a mother's heart.

ALICE.   But where is he? Surely you have brought him.

EDGAR.   Oh, he is here. And if I must say, I drew him such a picture of a little sister Alice I had that he was more anxious to get to Raby Castle than I was.

ALICE.   Edgar, what nonsense!

EDGAR.   But where is he loitering?

The crowd divides. ALAN RABY *is discovered, habited in the ordinary dress of the time. He is standing in the same spot as when first seen in Act One.*

Ah, here he is. Come, my dear fellow, let me present you to my mother and my sister. They are impatient to know and thank you. (ALAN *advances*) Lady Peveryl—Mr. Gervase Rookwood.[16] My sister Alice—Mr. Rookwood.

LADY P.   Oh, sir, I have indeed to thank you.

ALICE.   (*aside to* AUGUSTA) What a strange countenance.

AUG.   What a cold, icy look. I would not be alone in the dark with that man for my life.

EDGAR.   (*taking* AUGUSTA'*s hand*) And here is my cousin.

AUG.   Don't, don't Edgar! Please—if he only looks at me with those great black eyes, I shall shut up into my hoop like a telescope. (EDGAR *laughs and up remonstrating with her L.H.*)

ALICE.   With what a strange sentiment this man inspires me. He seems to possess already a mysterious power over me for which I cannot account. 'Tis a fascinating fear which attracts me. Oh, this is the folly of an overwrought imagination.

ALAN RABY *moves from* LADY PEVERYL *and addresses* ALICE. *She visibly gets trembles before him. He appears to exercise a mysterious domination over her. They sit on the settee.* EDGAR, *who has come down with* AUGUSTA *R.H., joins* LADY PEVERYL.

AUG.   Did you ever see such a death-like face, aunt?

EDGAR.   Pray, do not seem to notice it—it annoys him. It is the result of a wound received long ago in some romantic affair. (LADY PEVERYL *goes up and is seen to give directions to the servants*) Now, Rookwood, that I have introduced you to the present generation of my relations, let me present you to the past—they are all here. (*points to the portraits*)

ALAN: Perhaps they are already known to me.

EDGAR.   By history, but not by sight. To you who know so well the history of the civil wars—yonder portraits will have a peculiar interest. Look! In the same frame you see the unfortunate Ralph and Owen Raby (ALAN *turns slowly and views the portraits*)—once the lords of this castle where we now stand. It was reduced to ruins under the Commonwealth,[17] but restored by my grandfather to whom the estate was granted by William the Third.[18]

LADY P.   Part of the ancient building still remains.

ALAN.   (*smiling*) Ay, madam, this room.

EDGAR.   Do not be surprised, mother, Rookwood is so deeply read in history and genealogy that his knowledge of the past is little short of miraculous. Yes, this room did form part of the ancient castle and so did a certain old clock tower which was likewise preserved for the beauty of the ruin.

ALAN.   Not so. It was preserved because around it is buried those ancestors whose portraits are in this room.

EDGAR.   (*to his mother*) Now he found that out in some musty old manuscript, Heaven knows when. Well, this handsome youth is Roland Peveryl of unhappy memory.

ALAN.   Why have you passed over one?

EDGAR.   That— (*points to the portrait of* LUCY) Poor girl! You know her fate. That, Rookwood, is Lucy Peveryl, who with her cousin Roland Peveryl met with a mysterious fate.

ALAN.   Ay, on this day one hundred years ago.

EDGAR.   On this day!

LADY P.   The 15th of August.

EDGAR.   It is so, indeed. I remember now. Her tomb is beside the old clock tower. Yes, it bears that date. What a singular coincidence.

ALAN.   It seems strange, indeed. But there is one portrait you have still omitted.

EDGAR.   Where?

ALAN.   That above the door.

EDGAR.   That portrait, Rookwood, has no name. It is, I believe, the likeness of a stranger who was slain by accident on that very night we speak of.

ALAN. (*rising*) Ha, a portrait of—

EDGAR. It was painted from a sketch taken, 'tis said, on the spot by Foulke Nevil of Greystock.

AUG. Ah! Here is something he did not know, it seems.

ALAN. Why is the face concealed by that veil?

EDGAR. It is a superstition in our family that there is an evil influence in it, and whosoever looks upon it is sure to meet with some calamity.

LADY P. Why do you smile, sir?

ALAN. Because, madam, with two ladies in the family you have surely discovered already that there is no truth in the legend.

LADY P. You think the temptation too strong for a woman's curiosity, yet I am convinced that curtain has never, during my life time, been withdrawn.

ALAN. I believe you, madam.

EDGAR. Had it not been specially provided in Lord Arthur Clavering's will that the portrait should be preserved and placed in this room, it would have been destroyed long ago.

AUG. I must say I should like to take a peep at it.

EDGAR. But see, mother, it is past nine o'clock—hasten the supper.[19] It will be the first time that Rookwood and I have eaten at the same board. (LADY PEVERYL *goes up and off*)

The parts of ladies and gentlemen return during the two preceding speeches.

AUG. (*aside*) Edgar, did you ever see a bird beneath the fascination of a snake? Look—see the face of Alice, how it quivers beneath his gaze. (ALICE *rises*)

EDGAR. Hush! Alice is a girl of romantic imagination. The cold, thoughtful character of Rookwood awes and captivates her.

ALAN *and* ALICE *walk slowly up to the window and remain during the ensuing scene, gazing out at the balcony which is bathed in the moonlight. Enter* WATTY RHYS.

WATTY: Master Edgar, hist sir, Master Edgar, may I come in?

AUG. Who is that?

WAT. My humble service to you, Miss Augusta.

EDGAR. Do you not remember Watty Rhys? Come, Watty.

WAT. Master Edgar, my family have served yours for more than a century.

EDGAR. Do you think if it were not for that circumstance I would put up with such an intolerable nuisance as you are?

WAT. When you went on the continent to travel in search of foreign parts, your dear mother gave you into my care. Sir, I shall never forget the moment—she was pasting the list of your linen inside the lid of your portmanteau and crying over each shirt as she folded 'em. Enough to give you death o' cold.

EDGAR. Will you tell me what you want and then go to the devil.

WAT. Yes, sir. I want a character. You can just say you've known me a hundred years—I mean my family. Yes, sir. And as for going to the devil, sir, 'taint no occasion, Master Edgar, the devil's come to us.

EDGAR. Do not mind him, Augusta, he has taken a foolish idea into his stupid Welsh dunderhead about my friend Rookwood.

AUG. Ah—

WAT. Yes, Miss, I know what I've seen. This here friend that gives himself for an Englishman is no Englishman.

AUG. But why not?

WAT. Because, miss, because if an Englishman had a wound right through his body, either he would die or the wound would heal—that's our maxim.

EDGAR. This folly again!

WAT. I tell you I saw it. Here near his heart, as if a pistol bullet had passed clean through him.

AUG. And what do you suppose from this?

WAT. I suppose, I suppose, that I have watched him narrowly for eighteen months and no food or drink has passed his lips. That ain't English. He never gave his hand to anyone—not even to Master Edgar. That ain't English. He never put his foot inside a place of worship. That ain't English. And when the stupid parlyvoos[20] didn't understand our lingo,[21] he didn't damn 'em up and down as you and I did. Sir, he ain't an Englishman; he's a foreigneering Beelzebub.[22]

AUG. Edgar, is this strange tale true?

EDGAR. For the wound he speaks of, need I answer, he is deceived. For the rest, Rookwood is of a strange, retiring nature, but that he exists not as other people is a chimera[23] of yonder addlepate.[24]

WAT. Miss Nevil, Miss, I have at home an old bedridden granny, who, when I was a boy, used to tell me stories of the old times. She had it from her father, Watkyn Rhys, who, like me, was a servant here.

AUG. What did she tell you?

WAT. She told me that Watkyn Rhys had often been heard to say that the stranger who was slain on the night when Lucy Peveryl and Roland were murdered—that this stranger was no other than Alan Raby.

EDGAR. Which only proves that addlebrains are hereditary in your family.

AUG. Go on, Watty.

WAT. And there's always been a sort of belief that Alan Raby still lives. And year after year on the 15th of August have I sat up to hear if the old clock tower would chime midnight—but it didn't; and granny said it would not until Alan Raby once more appeared in Raby Hall, which he would do day for day, hour for hour, a hundred years after the deed.

EDGAR. And this day just completes the century.

AUG. Edgar, there is something more than natural in this coincidence.

EDGAR. Augusta, listen, I owe my life to Rookwood, and shall I for the fantastic babbling of this idiot allow a suspicion to cross my mind at once so unmanly, ridiculous and degrading? (*to* WATTY) Down to the kitchen. If my service is not to your mind, begone!

WAT. Oh, Master Edgar! Oh, Master Edgar!

EDGAR. Well, there, there you old fool. I did not mean to hurt you. But no more of that—leave me.

WAT. I would lay down my life for anyone who bore your name, but still if I had to die tomorrow— (ALAN *and* ALICE *return*) I would say that Mr. Rookwood as you call him is—

ALAN. Well, friend, what am I? (WATTY *staggers back and runs off*)

EDGAR. (*laughing*) Come, let us join our friends in the supper hall.

EDGAR *and* AUGUSTA *go off laughing. Exeunt.*

ALICE. Believe me, sir, my brother in his letters could never say enough of your goodness, your nobility and genius. And we were never wearied of reading your praises. Oh, you are no stranger here.

ALAN. And I, I have heard your name ever allied to terms of endearment, never uttered but in the tones of love. I have lived in your presence, partaken in your thoughts and shared your life. Ay, I, the thirsting student, the stoic,[25] who had forsworn the world, surrounded by the great spirits of the past, living, I might say, with the dead—your image seemed to beckon me to life. In sorrow I dreamed that from your swimming eyes I quenched my thirst for knowledge in a deep draught of love; in sickness I dreamed that from your heart there flowed a stream in which I could revive my life.

ALICE. Forbear, sir—oh, forbear! I know not how to answer you.

ALAN. Avow the truth that trembles on your lips. My spirit has preceded me—I have been with you here—unknown. I have watched you, and you were long since marked for mine. You have confessed it, Alice, I am no stranger here.

ALICE. Yes, yes, I have known you as the friend, the preserver of my brother's life.

ALAN. And for him who so preserved your brother's life—

ALICE. Oh, I will give my own.

ALAN. I accept the gift. (ALICE *covers her face with her hand; a distant peal of laughter heard faintly from without*)

ALICE. Leave me. I know not what I say. My brain swims round. Your presence seems to paralyze me.

ALAN.   Thou art mine, Alice.

ALICE.   What terrible and fatal power envelopes me!

ALAN.   Thou art mine, Alice.

ALICE.   Away! Yes—yes—I am—I am thine for I am powerless. Be merciful—leave me, if but for a while that I may think—that I may weep. (*she weeps and falls with her head over left arm of couch*)

ALAN.   I obey. (*he retires*)

ALICE.   What have I done? Oh, there is some dread emotion twines about my heart and chokes its throb. Can this be love? No—no—it is a frenzied fascination. What did I avow? Not my love. No, My gratitude. Yet is it gratitude that makes me shudder thus? (*turning to portraits*) Oh, you ancestors of my race! Why do your eyes seek me with that mournful gaze? Why have you no tongues to tell me what is this spell—that—overpowers—me—thus—and leaves me—senseless—thus—oh!

She falls into a stupor on the settee. A pause. Darkness arrives slowly. The room gradually changes and returns to the ruined state as seen in the 1st Act. The portraits alone excepted. The frame of LUCY PEVERYL'*s portrait descends very slowly. The room is dimly illuminated by the moonlight, which comes through the window. But in that spot where* ALICE *lies on the settee, beside her on a small table is a shaded lamp which casts down a circle of light upon her face and figure.* LUCY PEVERYL *glides forward out of the picture frame.*

LUCY.   Roland—Roland, where art thou? The hour is come.

The moonlight is shed brilliantly upon the floor and crossing it diagonally gleams upon the picture of ROLAND *on the wall R.H. The portrait of* ROLAND *descends and advances to window.*

  Lords of Raby, oh, why loiter ye within your tomb?

The portrait of RALPH *and* OWEN RABY *descends during this and the ensuing scene.* LUCY *stands C., directing a steadfast, thoughtful gaze forward, never turning towards either of the figures addressed, and speaking in a mournful tone, not in the commanding voice of invocation.* ROLAND, *who is habited in black velvet and having very light hair flowing over his shoulders, advances a little and directs his gaze towards the window. The moonlight falls upon this figure.* RALPH *and* OWEN RABY *do not quit the frame, but merely change their attitudes. All this is done slowly. The veiled portrait remains unmoved. A distant peal of laughter faintly heard within.* LUCY *proceeds.*

The weary time has fled, and year succeeding year,
A hundred have been told. Th'appointed hour is near.
Too well the curse of Raby marks this fatal day,
   The Phantom[26] has returned to seek another prey.
A virgin of his race, who if she yields her heart,
Will with her ebbing life another life impart.
Another hundred years he will achieve, and doom
Our lives which live in him unto a living tomb.
Obstructed, uncontent, in earth we must remain,
While mortal lives like ours the phantom's life sustain. (*as she glides back to the portrait*)
Speed, moments, speed, oh haste the tardy midnight's chime,
that we may sleep in peace until the end of time.

The portraits rise and regain their position. The scene slowly becomes restored to its previous form. ALICE, *after a moment, wakes from her stupor and starts up.*

ALICE.   Oh, mercy, help! Help me! Ah! (*slips from the settee to her knees*) Where am I? (*a distant peal of laughter from the family within*) No, no, I am here still. Merciful powers protect me, 'twas but a dream—a dream—but, oh, how terrible. I was in a ruined chamber inhabited by those whose portraits are there. They seemed to commune with each other, and they spoke—of what I forget—let me recall my scared thoughts. What said they? No, I forget, I forget. Are they still there? (*looks slowly around*) Ay, all—all. And now they appear to fix a gaze upon me as they would speak. See—their eyes turn now away. Whither do they look? Ah, do my senses cheat me? They turn towards yonder veiled portrait and seem to bid me seek there the dread solution of this mystery. Ay, I remember that picture moved not when the others came; 'tis the likeness of the stranger who was slain on this night and in this place one hundred years ago. What can the fate of this man have to do with mine? I know not—a viewless hand impels me on—I must know more. (*she goes up and locks the door C. and after a moment's hesitation, she draws back the curtain from the portrait and discovers the likeness of Rookwood*) Ah! 'Tis he! 'Tis he! My dream comes back. I remember they spoke of one hundred years that had elapsed, and then the phantom had returned to seek another prey. Oh! This cannot be—I must be mad—I dream still! (*the secret panel opens and reveals the staircase in the wall as seen in Act One.* ALAN RABY *enters*)

ALAN.   Alone! (*he advances and stands beside her*)

ALICE.   (*not seeing him*) Yet their last words still ring in my ear: 'Speed, moments, speed and hasten midnight's chime'. (*distant laughter faintly heard; she rises from the half-kneeling position in which she was*) Oh, these thoughts will madden me. I will seek Edgar.

ALAN. Stay.

ALICE. (*recoils*) You—you here.

ALAN. I found that door fastened so I came by yonder secret stair.

ALICE. There is—there is an unnatural influence about this man.

ALAN. Why do you look thus upon me, Alice?

ALICE. His form radiates a deadly cold.

ALAN. Alice, my own, for thou art mine—thou hast yielded up thy heart to me.

ALICE. (*retreating as he advances*) Ah, those words.

ALAN. Why dost thou recoil from me, Alice? Alice, speak to me and look not thus. We are alone—alone—none to hear thy voice but me. None to see thy blush proclaim the heart from which it comes is mine. Let me hold thee to my heart let my heart speak to thine—why dost thou repulse me?

ALICE. Because that breast on which you press me seems to be the bosom of a corpse and because from the heart within I feel no throb of life.

He starts towards her. She recoils.

ALAN. (*aside*) Betrayed—discovered—but how? (*turns and sees the portrait*) Ha! The portrait!

EDGAR. (*without*) Alice! Alice!

ALICE. My brother, ah! (*going up*)

ALAN. (*intercepting her*) Peace. Thou art mine. It is too late.

ALICE. Too late!

ALAN. Thy heart thou hast yielded to me. It is mine.

ALICE. Away, phantom! Demon! I know thee now.

ALAN.   Mine, mine. In thee is bound my life.

EDGAR.   (*without*) Alice! Alice! (*knocks at the door*)

ALICE.   My voice is choked with fear.

Retreats towards the door R.H. The chamber of LUCY *in the preceding act.*

ALAN.   Alice, thou art mine. (*advancing towards her*)

ALICE.   (*still retreating*) Avaunt![27] Away!

ALAN.   (*still advancing*) Mine.

EDGAR.   (*shaking the door*) Alice! Alice!

ALICE.   (*disappearing into the room*) No! No! Abhorrent spectre!

ALAN.   Thou art mine.

Follows her. A pause.

EDGAR.   (*without*) Alice! Open—open, Alice! (*the door is thrust open; he advances*) I heard her voice—in fear—entreaty. Rookwood too has disappeared. This door fastened—a shapeless terror haunts me. Alice! Alice! Where is she? (*turns and sees the portrait*) Ah, 'tis he! 'Tis Rookwood! Oh, what horror. Rookwood and this stranger—the same. Merciful providence! The fears of Watty Rhys I treated as mad folly. Can the legend then be true? It is, and Alice, my sister, where is she? Alice! Alice! Oh, she is here. (*as he rushes towards the door of the chamber,* ALAN RABY *appears in the doorway; the turret clock begins to chime midnight*) Demon! Where is my sister? Ah! (*draws his sword as* ALAN RABY *steps back*) She is dead! Fiend! Back to thy native hell!

ALAN *steps behind him and places his hand on his head.* EDGAR *stretches out his arms. The sword escapes from his hand. He utters a groan and falls as if the hand had struck death into his brain.* ALAN RABY *steps back into the balcony.*

ALAN.   Once more my cup of life is full. A hundred years of respite from perdition. Ye fated halls of Raby—till then—farewell!

Act Drop.

Characters in the Third Drama

Sir Alan Raby
Charles Peveril
Walter Rees, Attorney at Law
Postman
Mrs. Raby
Ada

The Third Drama

SCENE ONE

Time: the 15th of August, 1860. Scene: The town of Raby Peveril. Evening. The site is the same as seen in the first scene of the First Drama. A few objects remain to identify the spot, which is now covered with a modern and neatly built small town. The village church remains as before, and the house L.H. which was Owen Griffith's *inn has now become a private residence. On the door of which, facing the audience, is a large brass plate on which is engraved, 'Walter Rees, Attorney at Law'.* Walter Rees *is discovered in a bow window of the ground floor, writing at a desk. The window is open. Enter a* Postman *from back. He knocks at* Rees's *door.*

Rees.   (from the window) Here!

Post.   Walter Rees, Esq.

Rees.   That's me—Esquire.[1]

Post.   One and eightpence.[2]

Rees.   One and eightpence—what for—a letter? *(he disappears from window and enters from door)* What's in the letter—a ton of coals? *(he takes the letter)* There. *(gives money; exit* Postman*)* Who can my one and eightpence correspondent be? Where are my spectacles? *(searches)*

Enter Captain[3] Peveril. *He looks about.*

Pev.   The place is so changed, I can scarcely recognize the village of Raby Peveril. *(sees* Walter Rees*)* Oh, I pray, sir, can you inform me?

Rees.   Yes, sir, I can. But let me warn you that I am an attorney—if you can afford a conversation with me, go on. You have the fear of the law before your eyes.

Pev.   *(aside)* 'Tis he, 'tis Watty Rees himself. He does not know me.

REES. Come. Service for service. You have lost your way, and I have lost my spectacles. Read me the signature to that letter and I'll put you on your road.

CAPTAIN PEVERIL *takes letter.*

PEV. (*aside*) My own letter. (*aloud*) It comes from the headquarters of her Majesty's army of occupation in Burmah.[4]

REES. I wish her Majesty's army of occupation in Burmah would pay their postage—one and eightpence.

PEV. It is signed Charles Peveril.

REES. Charles—Charlie Peveril.

PEV. It announces his leave of absence and his immediate arrival in England. (*returns the letter to* WALTER REES)

REES. Give it to me—let me read—where are my spectacles? Hollo—the seal unbroken. (CAPTAIN PEVERIL *laughs*) And yet you know the contents. What are you, a conjuror?[5]

PEV. No, only a captain in her Majesty's service.

REES. A cap—stay—no, let me look at you. It is not Char—it isn't—Damn me, where are my spectacles? Stop there. (*runs to window and takes the spectacles from his desk; comes forward putting them on*) Heh, heh, 'tis—'tisn't—yes—he! ho! 'Tis Charley Peveril! (*embraces him*) My dear boy!

PEV. My good old friend!

REES. How could you return in this way? Lord bless me, how glad I am. Let me look at you, let me—ho! ho! (*puts his spectacles up on his forehead, where they stick; he wipes his eyes*)

PEV. As happy and as kind as ever.

REES. Not a care above ground, thanks to the fortune your dear father left me. £90 a year![6]

PEV. Which added to what your business brings you—

REES. It makes exactly £90 a year.

THE THIRD DRAMA : SCENE ONE

PEV. (*laughing*) Does not the law thrive in Raby Peveril?

REES. Admirably! There has not been a case since I began practice, he! he! Whenever the boors here have a dispute, as I am the only lawyer here, I get both plaintiff and defendant, and having duly heard both sides, I give my opinion that they had best fight it out—he who wins at the tussle loses the law suit, so both are gainers.

PEV. But tell me—Mrs. Raby—my cousin, Ada—

REES. Ah, my dear boy, a sad change has come over the Rabys. You remember when you quitted us 15 years ago?

PEV. Could I forget how my departure brought the first tears that ever dimmed the blue eyes of Ada Raby—and clouded the bright face of her young mother.

REES. Ah, there are tears enough now, but no bright faces.

PEV. What d'ye mean?

REES. I mean that Mrs. Raby has turned serious[7] and ever since she found out that she was a lost sheep,[8] there has been no more backgammon[9] and toddy.[10]

PEV. And Ada?

REES. Ada, my dear boy, is an angel. I believe it was a mistake her ever coming into the world here at all.

PEV. Oh, I can see her!

REES. No you can't. I wish you could.

PEV. How?

REES. She is shut up—secluded they call it. They have darkened the poor child's mind and made her believe that the world is a snare of the devil's and everybody in it his imps[11] in disguise. They have frozen the smiles on her lip—the—the—the—

PEV. Demons!

REES. Yes, thank ye—they have taken all the curl out of her spirits.

43

Pev. Who has done this?

Rees. Hush! Mrs. Raby has got a serious friend. Who he is—where he comes from—no one dares to guess. But to judge by his looks, I should say he was a commercial traveller to a mourning establishment.

Pev. Oh, I arrive in time. I have written to Mrs. Raby to announce my return. She must have received my letter some weeks ago.

Rees. Then they have kept it a secret from Ada, for tonight she leaves England forever.

Pev. Leaves England!

Rees. Yes. Here is an order for post-horses[12] to be in readiness an hour before midnight. See—written by the serious friend. It came down from the Hall yesterday—he has found some place of seclusion for her abroad. I see his game—he fears your presence.

Pev. He? Who?

Rees. Who? Why the serious friend—Mr. Gervase Rookwood.

Pev. Rookwood!

Rees. Hush! Here comes the old lady. (*enter* Mrs. Raby)

Pev. 'Tis she—but how changed. Aunt, dear Aunt, do you not know me?

Mrs. R. Charles! Dear Charles, this is indeed a pleasure I can scarcely refrain from enjoying. But we received your letter; we are prepared.

Pev. Oh, Aunt, it is not so I hoped to have been welcomed.

Mrs. R. Years have worked a blessed change in me. I have wrestled with my worser part.[13]

Rees. (*aside to* Peveril) She alludes to the backgammon and toddy.

Pev. You are changed indeed.

Mrs. R. I was a lost sheep—wandering in the wilderness of iniquity.[14]

Pev. But Ada—I cannot believe what I have heard.

MRS. R. She has abjured[15] the vanities of life—her eyes are opened to this Babel of abomination.[16] She offers up her youth—a pious offering.

PEV. You call this piety? Oh, Madam, where is your mother's heart? Why, I have come from scenes of carnage where savage men made death their sport, yet there's not one of us—no, not one—who could in cold blood have led a gentle, unresisting girl to a living tomb, cheering her lingering death with admiration of her agony.

REES. (*aside*) I wish the serious friend were here.

PEV. But I will see her.

MRS. R. My dear Charles.

REES. (*aside*) Edge in a word about the toddy.

PEV. She will listen to me. Her heart will awake when she hears the accents of love.

MRS. R. Love—horror! What do I hear? You shall not see her—I forbid it. I am her mother.

PEV. You are no longer worthy of the name.

REES. Bravo.

MRS. R. Dare you invade my house?

PEV. Ay. Who can oppose me? (*enter* ALAN RABY *at the back*)

REES. (*seeing him*) The devil! (*he sneaks into the house and presently appears at the bow window*)

MRS. R. You come too late. Today she will be conveyed from here to a country where her seclusion will be protected.

PEV. Under your maternal guidance.

ALAN. No, sir, under my care.

PEV. Ah, who is this?

REES. (*leaning from the window*) That's the serious friend!

Pev. I feel in presence of an enemy—but never have I faced such a one before. He fills me to the throat with fear.

Alan. Captain Peveril: your return at such a moment I esteem an undeserved blessing. The interest you feel in our young friend becomes you. You shall see her—use your fondest eloquence—let us not deprive her of this occasion to achieve a victory of the flesh.

Pev. Vipers! Have you so poisoned her soul that you are so certain of the result?

Alan. You see, sir, I bear your insults meekly.

Pev. There is patience on your tongue, but defiance in your eyes—leave me.

Alan. Yet a word. One hour before midnight Ada Raby leaves her home under my guidance—never to return. She leaves it willingly. Her heart is yielded up to my persuasions—she breathes another life.

Pev. Begone!

Alan. I obey.

Mrs. R. Oh, Charles! How can you? (*goes up with* Alan *and off R.H.*)

Pev. No, it is impossible that Ada can resist my prayers. When I tell her that I have lived for her—what have been my hopes, my dreams—and to find her thus. And tonight she will be irrevocably lost to me. I will hasten at once to Raby Hall. (*re-enter* Rees)

Rees. Stop! Take me with you. They are two-to-one against you. I'll tackle the old woman.

Pev. But what pretence can I afford?

Rees. I have some business in an old oak coffer[17] which is in the room called Alan Raby's chamber.

Pev. I thought that room was nailed up and condemned two hundred years ago.

Rees. I opened it and discovered a coffer full of old manuscripts and deeds. I hope to find there some missing papers relating to your property.

PEV.   Come then. Her heart cannot be frozen. My tears will melt her resolution.

REES.   And I would dissolve the old lady—if I could but get her over a glass of toddy.

PEV.   Come.

Exeunt. REES *returns.*

REES.   Stop. I forgot my spectacles. (*runs to the window and takes his spectacles and hurries after* CAPTAIN PEVERIL)

SCENE TWO

The turret chamber. Decorated in a modern style. The portraits remain as before but in different frames—except that of the Vampire, in the place of which is a portrait of Alice. A clock with a practicable dial points to 10. Enter ADA *and* MRS. RABY.

ADA.   My dearest mother, do as you will with me. I am faint of spirit.

MRS. R.   We must separate, dear Ada, for a little while. Tonight, an hour before midnight, all will be in readiness. In a few weeks I will join you.

ADA.   Mother, it is not the world that I regret, but there is one I yearned to see—to say farewell to him.

MRS. R.   You mean Charles Peveril.

ADA.   Alas!

MRS. R.   Are you most certain, Ada, that, were he here, he might not still dissuade you from your blessed destiny?

ADA.   No, no!

MRS. R.   Would you most solemnly pledge yourself that his prayers, entreaties, even tears will not affect you?

ADA.   What do you mean? He *is* here.

MRS. R.   Promise me, Ada.

ADA. I do, I do. But speak! (*enter* PEVERIL *followed by* REES)

PEV. Ada, dear Ada!

ADA. Ah!

MRS. R. Be firm.

ADA. Charles, I—I—am (*covers her face with her hands*)

PEV. Ada, Ada, do you not know me?

ADA. I do—I do! (*she is clasped in his arms*)

REES. What a picture! Where are my spectacles? (*searches*)

MRS. R. Ada, you forget your promise.

PEV. Take mine, Madam. Leave me but one hour to say farewell.

MRS. R. An hour. Be it so. (*looks at clock*) It is now 10 o'clock.

REES. So late.

MRS. R. At eleven you part.

PEV. Forever.

REES. Till then I have some papers to examine in yonder chamber.

MRS. R. (*aside*) I will warn our friend. His succour to the feeble may be needful. I see she is in peril.

Exits. REES *crosses to L.H. door, but when* MRS. RABY *has gone off, he creeps over to the clock.*

REES. She allows you one hour. See, Charley, I'll give you another—so—I put back the clock. (*he puts back the hands of the clock from 10 to 9*) From 10 to 9. So when they think 'tis but eleven it will be midnight. There, make the most of your time; and if you don't make a lost sheep of her again you deserve to be cashiered. (*exits into L.H. room*)

PEV. Ada, speak to me. Have you indeed resolved to leave me?

ADA. I never felt till now how strangely I am changed from what I was. Yes, Charles, I feel an urging spirit in me that hurries me towards my destiny.

PEV. Do you know that I have loved you, Ada? Yes, from your childhood. I bore your image with me when we parted—years passed by—I loved you still. Hope inspired me and I saw you as I see you now—clasped in my arms, confessing in return a love as deep.

ADA. Charles, spare me. I dare not listen more.

PEV. You shall, Ada, if not for your sake, hear me for mine. I plead for my life, for my happiness.

ADA. I dare not yield and yet my heart rebels.

PEV. You seem as if you struggled with a spell.

ADA. Yes, it is so. He is my master, I cannot avoid him.

PEV. Rookwood!

ADA. Hush! When he is away I determine to resist his power. But then he comes, his influence creeps like a shadow slowly over me and I am helpless.

PEV. (*aside*) Her mind wanders.

ADA. Take me. Take me from them, Charles. (*throws herself into his arms*)

PEV. Thou will be mine, Ada.

ADA. Yes—yes. I see now the fate for which they destined me. Shield me!

PEV. Come then—let me see the power that can take you from my arms. Let us leave this place.

ADA. I cannot. (*she stands as if spellbound*)

PEV. How?

ADA. He comes! He comes!

PEV. (*looks around*) No, we are alone.

ADA. You see him not; but I feel his presence.

Pev. Ada, be calm. (Alan *appears at back*)

Ada. Do you not see him now? (Alan *advances*)

Alan. (*fixing his eyes on* Ada *but speaking to* Peveril) The hour, sir, is come. (Ada *becomes statue-like under his gaze*)

Pev. Ay, the hour of freedom for your victim.

Alan. (*aside*) I arrive in time.

Pev. She will not doom to misery those she loves. She has appealed to me to shield her from your power.

Alan. (*aside*) Ada!

Pev. Let me see who dares to tear her from the refuge she has sought within my arms.

Alan. (*withdrawing his eyes from* Ada) Be it so, sir, she is free to go. (*steps back a pace*)

Pev. Ada, come, dear Ada. Why this silence?

Alan. Listen. (*addressing himself to her*) You hear, Ada? Speak.

Ada. (*mechanically*) Yes, I hear.

Alan. Do you repent the destiny you have chosen?

Ada. No!

Alan. Will you, at once, quit this spot and fly to the seclusion I have found for you?

Ada. I will.

Alan. Freely.

Ada. Yes.

Alan. You demand no protection but mine.

Ada. None.

PEV.   Ada, what do I hear? Ada, unsay these cruel words! Did you not implore my aid? To shield thee from a horrid fate?

ALAN.   You did not say this, Ada.

ADA.   No.

PEV.   Oh! What mystery is this? Ada! She does not hear me.

ADA.   Oh, release me! Oh, I am in torture!

PEV.   Ada!

ALAN.   (*aside to him*) Do you not see, sir, this woman is mad.

PEV.   (*recoiling*) Mad!

ALAN.   We would have spared your feelings, but you would know the truth. You found a sad change worked in those you left so happy.

PEV.   Mad!

ALAN.   Can you not guess, then, the seclusion for which she is destined?

PEV.   (*gazing at* ADA) Here is the cause. Oh, pardon, pardon, sir. You know not how I loved her. (*he buries his face in his hands*)

ALAN.   (*aside*) She is mine.

ADA.   (*in a low tone and mechanically as if echoing his thought*) I am thine.

ALAN.   The night is far advanced, sir. (*looks to the clock; it marks 10*) Ha! (*goes towards the clock*)

PEV.   Ada—farewell!

ADA.   (*abstractedly*) Farewell.

PEV.   Ada, is it thus we part?

ADA.   (*recovering and rising*) We part.

PEV.   Speak one word—I will watch over you—protect you still.

ADA. Why do you look thus upon me? Why do you weep? What have I done? (*throws her arms around* PEVERIL)

ALAN *advances. Her eyes, wandering, meet his.*

ALAN. Ada! (*her arm falls from* PEVERIL's *shoulder*)

PEV. One word—speak one word!

ALAN. (*in a low voice to her*) Farewell.

ADA. Farewell.

PEVERIL *goes up to the table and throws himself in the chair beside it and leans his face upon his hands.*

ALAN. (*receding toward the door R.H.*) Ada!

She turns towards him; he disappears slowly by the door R.H.

(*without*) Ada! (*she follows him*)

The scene closes in.

SCENE THREE

ALAN RABY's *chamber. A bedroom of the 17th century. The hangings and decorations moth-eaten and decayed. Every sign of desolation. The furniture and clothing scattered about the room to show that it remains as* ALAN RABY *left it. Enter* REES, *a candle in one hand and dragging after him a great oaken coffer.*

REES. Here it is—just as I left it thirty years ago when I made the inventory. They say this room is haunted with bad spirits. I'll try—on a shelf there I found a bottle of something mysterious. (*opens coffer, pulls back the lid and sits on the edge; takes an old fashioned glass bottle and glass*) I'll exorcise the devil. (*takes out the stopper and pours himself a glass; drinks*) I wish I may be haunted by this bottle imp[18] every night. (*drinks again*) Hollands—two hundred years in bottle.[19] (*searches in the chest and draws out papers*) What have we here? Tenure of the lands of Glasslyn[20]— Henry VII.[21] Pooh. How old it smells. (*picks out another*) Llandwrog[22] title and manorial right. Jetsam and flotsam[23]—no—what ruffians those Middle Age barons were.[24] They took whatever came under their hands— (*drinks*) —just as if it were their own. (*picks out another bundle of papers*)

Edgar Peveril—correspondence—July 19, 1760—a hundred years ago! (*reads another paper*) To Lieutenant General Oliver Cromwell. Law! A letter to Cromwell! (*opens it*) And signed! Oh! (*he puts down the glass*) Oh, Lord, it can't be! (*goes to look again but checks himself, fills up a bumper and drinks it*) Now for it. (*takes the candle and looks at the letter*) Alan Raby. Yes, not a letter wanting. July 16, 1645—written just after the murder of his brothers. What a curious document. (*examines it*) How very odd. I could swear I had seen this handwriting somewhere. That 'g' now, who the devil is it makes his 'g's like that? Who can it be? It isn't our parson, no! Stop, it's Old Wynne—no—let me remember. (*he is raising the glass to his lips when it flashes across his mind*) Eh—oh—yes—Egod—it is—the—the—the serious friend! I'm sure of it, the very same. Oh, Lord, what's the matter with me, I'm all of a shake. Oh! It can't be—Walter Rees, don't be an old fool. Damme, sir, hold up! It can't be, sir, I tell you, stop—here! (*pulls out his pocket book*) Where's the order for the post-horses? (*he draws out a paper and compares it with the letter*) It can't be—no—it—it cannot. He—he—he! Damned if it isn't. Oh, I feel every hair in my head is turning grey! Let me think—let me recall the legend. I heard it regularly told by my poor father every 15th of August when he used to drink 'Death to the Curse of Raby'—the 15th of August—why, 'tis today! And the name of the travelling companion of Edgar Peveril—my father always called him Alan Raby, but he bore another name. It began with an 'R'—stay—I saw a bundle of Edgar's letters. (*hastily searches; selects one and reads*) Florence. 1st of July, Old Style, 1760. 'My dearest Mother, you may surely expect me at old Raby Hall on the 15th of August next—my birthday. I am most anxious to see you to present to you my valued friend, Mr. —'

He drops the letter and seizes the bottle of spirits, which he drains. Falls back into the box. Enter Mrs. Raby.

Mrs. R.   Mr. Rees! I am truly astonished!

Rees.   Is that all—come here—come—and let me horrify you. Take a seat. (*points to the other corner of the bed and the coffer*)

Mrs. R.   He is intoxicated.

Rees.   I wish I was. I am not so happy, my dear friend. I have made a curdling discovery—hush!

Mrs. R.   (*sitting*) You terrify me.

Rees.   Answer me: do you know that there is a legend attached to your family?

Mrs. R.   You mean the curse of Raby!

Rees.   What is the date on the tomb of Lucy Peveryl, still extant beneath the old clock tower?

Mrs. R.   The 15th of August, 1660.

Rees.   On what day was Alice Peveril found murdered?

Mrs. R.   The 15th of August, 1760.

Rees.   And today—today is the 15th of August, 1860. Just day for day a hundred years apart.

Mrs. R.   What do you mean?

Rees.   Today the curse is due. Tonight, ere the old clock tower chimes midnight, the phantom must appear to seek a third victim.

Mrs. R.   What do you mean?

Rees.   I mean that he has come—he is here.

Mrs. R.   He—he—whom?

Rees.   Look, do you know that writing? (*hands her Alan Raby's letter*)

Mrs. R.   Yes—'tis Rookwood's.

Rees.   You are sure?

Mrs. R.   Certain!

Rees.   Look at the signature.

Mrs. R.   (*reads*) Alan Raby! He—he—

Rees.   Look here. This letter of Edgar Peveril's to his mother—dated one hundred years ago. How does he call his friend?

Mrs. R.   (*reads*) Gervase Rookwood.

Rees.   Ay. The same who disappeared from this house on the night of Alice Peveril's death—when Edgar was found beside her corpse a raving maniac—the same who now—

Mrs. R. Ada! Ada, my child! (*she faints*)

Rees. (*supporting her*) Don't—don't give way, Mrs. Raby, don't. And there's no more in the bottle. (*enter* Peveril) Quick, Charley.

Mrs. R. (*recovering*) Save—save my child. Speak—I left her with you. Ada. Where is she?

Pev. She is gone.

Mrs. R. Gone.

Pev. With Rookwood.

Mrs. R. 'Tis not too late. Their departure was fixed for midnight. 'Tis just eleven—I saw the clock as I entered.

Rees. But I put it back an hour.

Mrs. R. Then she is lost!

Pev. Lost—speak, Madam. What mean you?

Mrs. R. I mean the curse of Raby is upon us. Ada is the victim.

Pev. Rookwood!

Mrs. R. The fiend. The Phantom. The murderer of Lucy Peveryl.

Pev. Demon! And I knew him not. Away! I saw her descend with him towards the ruins of the old clock tower—Man, fiend, or phantom I will save her or will share her fate.

He rushes out followed by Mrs. Raby.

Rees. Stop! Stop for me! Alarm the servants!

Exit Rees *after drawing after him the chest.*

SCENE FOUR

Mountainous country. The clock tower discovered. A large sarcophagus tomb,[25] on which is written, 'To the Memory of Lucy Peveryl who departed this life on the 15th of August, 1660'. ALAN RABY *discovered descending. He bears* ADA *in his arms. They cross the bridge, then* ALAN *throws it over the precipice. He advances and places her upon a knoll.*

ALAN.   Again I triumph. She is in my power. At midnight ends my demon-gifted life. At midnight a hundred years will once more have passed, and once again a pure untainted life drawn into mine will yield to me a century. Ada—arise.

ADA.   I am here.

ALAN.   Dost thou give thy heart up to me?

ADA.   I am powerless.

ALAN.   Why dost thou tremble thus?

ADA.   Because I know thee, Alan Raby. Thy deadly spirit haunts me. Thy power enfolds me. Is there no aid?

ALAN.   None human can avail thee now.

ADA.   Then Heaven have mercy upon me!

PEV.   (*without*) Ada! Ada! (ALAN *approaches her*)

ADA.   Phantom avaunt! Behold the tombs where lie your victims. Alice (*R.H.*) Lucy (*C.*). From your graves rise up and help, protect me.

ALAN.   Invoke their aid, for none human can avail you now.

ADA.   He comes—avoid thee demon!

ALAN.   He comes too late.

PEV.   (*on rocks*) Ada, I come! Ah, the bridge cut down.

ALAN.   Thou art mine. (*the turret clock chimes midnight*) My life, my life ebbs fast. Ha! The hour has come. Oh, malediction! Mercy! Mercy!

ALAN *starts back. The lid of* LUCY PEVERYL's *sarcophagus flies open. The bottom of the tomb rises with* LUCY *upon it. She stretches forth her arm, and places her hand upon* ALAN's *shoulder. He utters a cry and disappears into the tomb, which closes over him. At the time that* LUCY's *tomb opens,* ALICE *appears in ruined tomb R.H. As* ALAN *disappears L.H. they both sink again and their tombs close up.* PEVERIL *bounds across the chasm and catches* ADA *fainting in his arms.* MRS. RABY, REES *and servants bearing torches come on at the back amongst the rocks. Tableau.*[26]

Curtain.

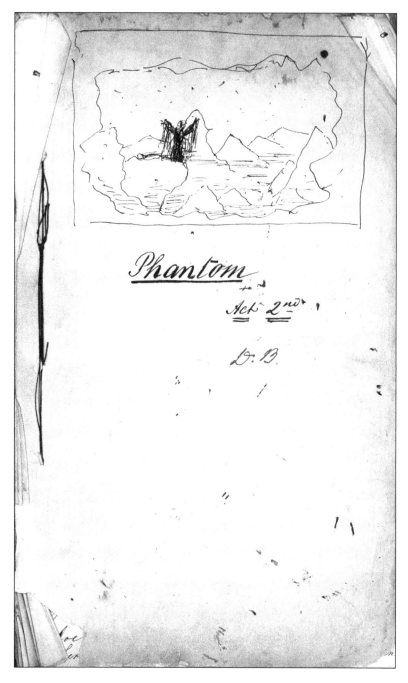

Figure 3. First page of Act II of Boucicault's 1852 script for *The Phantom* (MS-P). Courtesy University of South Florida Libraries Special Collections, Dion Boucicault Theatre Collection.

The Phantom, a Play in Two Acts

[THE 1873 REVISED MANUSCRIPT]

Characters in Act One, Period 1645

Sir Alan Raby
Lord Albert Clavering
Sir Guy Musgrave
Sir Hugh Nevil of Greystock
Ralph Gwynne
Davy
Servants
Lucy Peveril
Ellen Musgrave
Maud
Janet

Act One

SCENE ONE

Enter Janet with a basket on her arm.

JANET. Ho! Davy, stable the pony and give her a good feed, d'ye hear? Now let me count my marketing. (*examines contents of basket*) 6 bottles of good wine, a piece of brawn,[1] two white loaves, and a cheese, there, my larder is finally stocked. (*calls*) Master Roland. Master Roland. (*enter* DAVY)

DAVY. You got under shelter just in time mistress, for here comes the wildest thunderstorm of the year. Snowdon[2] has put on his black cap; 'twill be a wild night.

JANET. Where is our guest?

DAVY. He went up the mountain two hours ago.

JANET. What took him abroad in such weather?

DAVY. Colonel Peveril[3] and a party of Royal Horse[4] passed down the road two hours ago. Behind them troopers were found six pensioners,[5] Puritan[6] soldiers on their road to the gallows. Poor devils! Had they suspected that Captain[7] Claire was hiding in this place, they would have added him to their butcher's bill.

JANET. Turn, and turnabout is fair play, Davy. Ten years ago the Roundheads hung the Cavaliers.[8]

DAVY. Ay, every dog has his day.[9]

JANET. Hark! I hear a clatter on the road below. 'Tis master Roland returned.

DAVY. Nay 'tis the hoof of a horse—the captain went away on foot. (*looking out*) 'Tis a lady.

JANET. (*looking out*) Miss Lucy Peveril, the colonel's daughter, the storm has driven her to seek shelter here. Go hold her horse Davy. (*exit* DAVY) Take care, miss, how you alight. So, you are dearly welcome. Miss, pray come in. (*enter* Lucy)

Lucy. My father has gone to Llanberis[10] with a troop of horse,[11] has he passed down the road?

Janet. Some hours ago, Miss.

Lucy. When the road to Corwen is clear, my cousin Roland can escape tonight. Where is he?

Janet. Alarmed at the approach of your father's troopers, he left the house two hours ago, and sought some hiding place in the mountains. (*thunder*)

Lucy. I know where to find him. He foresaw this danger and appointed a spot above in the rook where we had often wandered when we were children.

Janet. But you surely will not venture to climb up there in the dark.

Lucy. I know every pebble in the road. My anxiety for Roland's safety banishes all fear for my own. (*re-enter* Davy)

Davy. Mistress! Good Lord, Mistress!

Janet. What's the matter? Why the man's face is as white as his shirt, whiter than his shirt.

Davy. There is a light in the ruins of Raby Castle.

Lucy. 'Tis Roland! That is the spot he appointed for our meeting.

Janet. Raby Castle. Do you not know the fearful character of that place?

Lucy. He cannot be in more danger amongst the lawless men who may seek shelter there, than he will be in this house on the King's highway,[12] for a price is set up on his head. So every passenger becomes a hired assassin. I will join him there at all hazards. He must leave England tonight. The vessel which bears him to France will sail at daybreak. (*thunder*)

Davy. Wait until the storm has passed. The tracks will be knee deep and floods, a goat could not hold his footing.

Lord C. (*outside*) Hillo! House, landlord!

ACT ONE : SCENE ONE

NEVILL AND RALPH. (*outside*) Hello, hostler!¹³

DAVY. (*looking out*) Ho! what a crowd of grand people. Our yard is full of nobles and ladies. Where shall we stable all their cattle?

LUCY. Strangers here.

Enter LORD CLAVERING, NEVIL, RALPH GWYNNE, MAUD, ELLEN, MUSGRAVE, *and* SERVANTS.

LORD C. Lead our horses under the shed. Do not fear, Lady Maud, these mountain storms are as brief as they are violent.

DAVY. It is in for the night, my Lord. It may let up for an hour, but if so the water courses will overflow, and the roads become impassable.

LORD C. We are besieged then by the elements.

NEVIL. We must camp out.

MAUD. But we are quite unprovided, what will they think at home if we do not return? (*thunder*)

NEVIL. The storm will speak for itself.

ELLEN. How provoking.

LORD C. Faith, there is but scant room in this shanty¹⁴ to accommodate our party. What can you do for us, hostess?

JANET. The best I can my Lord will be poor enough. The two rooms upstairs will suit these ladies, this chamber is at your service. Your servants can have the lofts over the stable.

LORD C. (*pointing at* LUCY) But you have another guest, this lady.

LUCY. (*rising and withdrawing her veil*) Lord Clavering.

LORD C. Miss Lucy Peveril!

MAUD AND ELLEN. Lucy!

LUCY. My cousin Roland, my betrothed, is here. I dare not tell my father that, for days he has been concealed in this neighborhood, seeking an occasion to bid me farewell, ere he left England forever. I cannot explain my presence here without betraying into your hands a proscribed and wretched fugitive whose life is forfeit to the royal cause.

Lord C. Captain Roland Claire is a worthy gentleman. We are not officers of the law, and shall rejoice to hear of his escape.

Lucy. To your honor I confide his life. He awaits me in the ruins of Raby.

Lord C. We will escort you there, for it must not be said that the daughter of Colonel Peveril met her lover in solitude.

Nevil. Why should we not pass the night there? There is still shelter in the ruined chambers.

Sir Guy. Aye, why should we not take up provisions and make a night of it?

Davy. I will tell you, because no one ever sought a night shelter in the ruins of Raby Castle that ever lived to see the morning.

All. How?

Janet. It is true.

Davy. A terrible mystery dwells there.

Nevil. It is a den of robbers?

Davy. No, the poor devils that have been found there were not murdered for their gold.

Sir Guy. Murdered!

Davy. Listen, gentlemen, within the ruins of Raby Castle dwells some terrible thing, man or fiend. (*thunder*) Oh Lord!

Lord C. Speak out, man.

Davy. No traveler that knows the road will ever venture near that spot after nightfall; but strange wayfarers benighted in the storm have wandered to its fatal shelter and next morning they are found—

Lord C. Dead!

Davy. Each with a wound in his throat but no blood is spilt around. The face is white and fixed, as if it had died in horror. (*thunder*)

LUCY.   And he, my betrothed, Roland, is there.

LORD C.   Can you lend credence to such a story?

LUCY.   I know not, but a feeling of terror creeps over me.

SIR GUY.   So it does over me.

NEVIL.   What say you gentlemen, does not this story prick your curiosity?

MAUD.   It will be delightful; the gentlemen can sit up and guard us. Quite romantic! A haunted castle.

DAVY.   It will be like sleeping in a stable full of nightmares.

LUCY.   Let us not delay, the storm holds off.

NEVIL.   But who is to guide us to the spot?

JANET.   Here's Davy, he will do it gladly.

DAVY.   Me! Do you want me to get my throat cut?

LORD C.   (*looking out*) The storm has abated, the rain has ceased for the moment. Let us avail ourselves of this lull in the tempest. 'Tis but an hour's brisk walk. Ho! Prepare torches there.

JANET.   Here are provisions, Sir, and all you need.

NEVIL.   'Tis an ill wind blows nobody any good, but this storm has blown us a charming adventure. I would not have missed such a night as this for a thousand pounds.[15]

DAVY.   Everyone to his task.

JANET.   There are cups, candles, knives, forks—dash where are the spoons?

DAVY.   Give them the long ones, they are going to sup with the devil.

SIR GUY.   Come shoulder the basket and show us the road.

DAVY.   Not for a crown piece would I go up the mountain tonight. You can't mistake the road, there's only one track, and if you miss your footing, as 'tis like you will, you will only meet your death over the precipice instead of in the ruins. What's the odds?

NEVIL.   Does the fellow refuse to serve as a guide? (*holding up a gold piece before* DAVY's *eyes*) Do you know what that is?

DAVY.   Yes, it's a guinea.[16]

NEVIL.   Lead up to the gates of the castle and there you shall be dismissed and you can return.

JANET.   A golden guinea.

LUCY.   You shall descend the mountain with Captain Claire, and if you follow him to Corwen and report to me his safety on board the ship, I will add fifty guineas.

JANET.   Fifty guineas. (*aside to* DAVY) Davy, I am yours.

DAVY.   Eh, what do you mean?

JANET.   Take the basket, earn the money like a man, and come back and ask me what I mean.

NEVIL.   She means to marry you, you dog, she wants to share your good fortune.

DAVY.   Fifty-one guineas, for a night's work. I'll do it. (*exeunt*)

SCENE TWO

The ruins of Raby Castle. C. arch. Set doors R. and L.H. A hat and rapier leans against flat L.H. Table and benches R.H. Enter RALPH GWYNNE *holding a torch. He ascends the stairway at back.*

RALPH.   Hillo! This way! Follow me.

NEVIL, SIR GUY, MAUD *and* SERVANTS *and* ELLEN, *ascend stair and advance.*

NEVIL.   Bravo! this chamber will serve us for a supper room—the roof is good.

MAUD.   Where is Lord Clavering?

LORD C.   Hillo!

ACT ONE : SCENE TWO

ELLEN.   Here he comes!

Enter LORD CLAVERING *and* LUCY.

LORD C.   What a strange place.

LUCY.   Where is he, where is Roland?

RALPH.   We have searched the ruins in every part except this floor.

LUCY.   He is not here.

NEVIL.   (*looking into chamber L.H.*) Here is a room, how dismal. There goes an old owl out at the window.

RALPH.   (*looking in R.H. chamber*) This is a bedchamber. Yonder is a gloomy looking couch.

SIR GUY.   Hallo! What's here? Somebody has recently occupied this room. Here is a hat and rapier.[17]

LORD C.   Let me see them.

LUCY.   'Tis Roland's sword. See, there is his cypher[18] on the hilt.

LORD C.   Calm your fears, he cannot be far. You see he has gained the castle; he is sheltering somewhere in its vast ruins.

LUCY.   Pardon me, but I feel a presentiment of some terrible calamity. It weighs upon my heart, as if some evil had befallen him.

LUCY *and* LORD CLAVERING *go up to window in flat. The servants lay the table R.H.*

SIR GUY.   What a dismal hole!

ELLEN.   It is not romantic.

NEVIL.   Where is the supper? Where is Davy? (*enter* DAVY *with basket*)

DAVY.   (*very pale*) Here I am in a cold perspiration. I am sure my hair must be turning grey. My heart feels like a jelly.

NEVIL.   Here, give us the supper.

Davy. Take it and let me say my prayers before I'm murdered.

Lord C. (*waving torch*) Roland! Roland!

Davy. Lord, what's that?

Ralph. Fools! It's only Lord Albert calling from the balcony for young Roland Claire.

Davy. I thought it was the devil calling for me.

Lucy. Roland! Roland!

Nevil. There, all is ready. Come, Lord Albert.

Lord C. Fear not dear lady, your betrothed hath wandered from the path and is sheltered in some mountain cave.

Ellen. The storm is passing. He will soon be here.

Lucy. No, no, a feeling of terror clings to my heart. But do not let me detain you from supper[19] or spoil your festivities.

Lord C. Will you not join us?

Lucy. Oh! Pardon me. I cannot.

Lord C. Away then. Davy, guide our servants to the room above, and prepare some shelter where the ladies may sleep.

Davy. Sleep! Oh Lord, what strong minded women they must be who could sleep in the ruins of Raby Castle. (*exit with servants*)

Nevil. And while we sup, let one of our party mount guard upon yonder stairway, I will take the post as sentinel. (*stands C. at back*)

Lord C. Come ladies, bumpers. Why Musgrave, you look pale. You actually tremble. Have you caught the fears of that booby.[20]

Sir Guy. No, no, only caught cold in my head.

Lord C. Our adventure tonight reminds me of a strange story, attached to a ruined castle in Germany.

All. Let us hear it.

ACT ONE : SCENE TWO

LORD C. It is a ghost story, ladies, and a fearful one I promise you. Fill and listen. It is now three years ago while traveling in Bohemia,[21] I passed just such a night as this, in the ruins of an old feudal castle which had the reputation of being haunted.

RALPH. By the murdered bride of some rascally old Baron?

LORD C. No, by a strange being called a vampire.

ALL. A vampire!

LORD C. Aye, the peasantry of the neighborhood declared that a phantom[22] of this kind inhabited the ruins and fed upon the benighted travelers who caught shelter there.

SIR GUY. What the devil was it like?

LORD C. It was a human being who had died some fifty years before, but who had made a compact with the fiend[23] to revive him after death. By some terrible means, a false life was instilled into the corpse, which moves and speaks, but no warm blood circulated in the monster's veins, all within was still as death.

NEVIL. But on what does he live?

LORD C. On human blood! Upon the lives of others, he recruits[24] his terrible existence.

LUCY. He comes not. Oh Roland, my heart is sick with fear.

SIR GUY. Give me a bumper of Burgundy.[25]

RALPH. What a dreadful story, can it be true?

LORD C. True! Impossible. It is but the creation of a diseased brain.

NEVIL. Alert! I see a dark figure moving among the ruins below.

LORD C. It may be Roland.

LUCY. Roland!

NEVIL. As the flashes of lightning gleam upon him, he seems by his garb to be a Puritan. He mounts the ruined stair.

LORD C. To arms, gentlemen!

Enter ALAN RABY.

LORD C. Who art thou?

ALAN. I am a stranger benighted in the storm. I heard that a noble company had sought shelter here. I come to claim your hospitality.

ALL. A Puritan!

ALAN. Aye, a Puritan, one who has been your foe. (*thunder and lightning*) But on a night like this, may we not be at peace?

LORD C. You are welcome, Sir. (ALAN *advances*)

SIR GUY. What a strange figure.

NEVIL. Do you remark the unnatural pallor of his countenance?

LORD C. May we ask whom we have the honor to entertain?

ALAN. My name is Gervase Rookwood, a poor gentleman and a stranger in these mountains; in the darkness of the storm I lost the path and thus became a suppliant to your courtesy.

LORD C. We have just supped, Sir. I pray you be seated. I will hold you company. (*enter* DAVY) Now, Davy, kindle a fire, take our guest's hat and cloak and dry them.

DAVY. Yes my Lord. I tremble in every limb, at every turn in this infernal castle. I expect to find myself face to face with the spectre, with the— with the—the—the—Oh Lord! (*as* DAVY *takes* ALAN's *cloak, and as* ALAN *hands his hat,* DAVY *catches a glimpse of his face and staggers back*)

NEVIL. What's the matter?

DAVY. Sir, Sir, do you know this gentlemen?

NEVIL. No, do you?

DAVY. N—No—That is—Yes—I did—Oh! It cannot be.

NEVIL. What do you mean?

DAVY. (*looking at* ALAN) Ten years ago, the Lord of this castle, Sir Alan Raby, was slain in this very room. I saw him once when I was a child and he—he was exactly like—

SIR GUY. Who?

DAVY. (*recoiling*) No—N—Nobody!

LORD C. Pardon this fellow, Sir, his terror drives him crazy. This castle ten years ago was the scene of an unnatural murder. It belonged to Owen Raby, a noble Cavalier, who fought bravely for King Charles[26] while Alan Raby, his younger brother, espoused the cause of Cromwell[27] and became a Puritan.

DAVY. (*watching* ALAN) I saw him once. I remember his black plume and cloak—not blacker than his heart—his Bible hanging by chains from his belt and his sword in his gripe.

LORD C. Since the murder of Owen Raby by his brother, and the subsequent destruction of the castle by our troops, the peasantry imagined that the place is haunted.

DAVY. Yes, by the ghost of the murderer, who they say pursues his business upon all who seek shelter here.

LUCY. My Lord, pardon my importunity, but a shapeless terror haunts me, the presence of this stranger appalls me. His gaze chills my heart.

LORD C. Do not fear, you are safe with us. Come be advised, take some refreshment, you are weak.

NEVIL. Come Davy, relate to us the particulars of the murder.

DAVY. I dare say this gentleman knows all about it. (*aside*) If I could hear him speak, I think I would recognize Alan Raby's voice.

LORD C. It is now ten years ago since the deed was done. At midnight the castle was surprised by a party of Puritans, headed by the younger brother. The sleeping garrison were butchered.

DAVY. In yonder chamber Lord Owen Raby slept. (*points L.H.*) The mark of his blood is still upon the floor where he fell, run through the heart by his brother Alan.

SIR GUY. But the murderer met his doom.

LORD C. One year afterward, the castle was attacked and stormed by the Royalist forces, and the fratricide[28] was taken.

DAVY. Yes, in this very room they seized him by the neck and hurled him headlong from yonder window.

NEVIL. There is a precipice beneath of untold depth.

DAVY. Then they set fire to the castle and blew up the battlements. The next day search was made for Alan Raby's body on the rocks beneath, but no trace of it could be found.

LORD C. Let us thank heaven that civil war is ended, which arrayed brother against brother and father against son. Come ladies, I see that your place of rest for the night is prepared. Miss Peveril, you will occupy yonder apartment. (*points R.H.*) Gentlemen, the apartment beneath is at your service. I will remain in this room to keep watch, for although I do not believe in ghosts, I have a sound suspicion of robbers. So good night and pleasant dreams to all.

Exeunt all C.D. but LORD CLAVERING *and* DAVY. *Exit* LUCY *R.H.*

LORD C. Now Davy, leave me. I would pass the night alone. (*pointing L.H.*) There is the chamber yonder where you can sleep.

DAVY. That is Alan Raby's bedroom.

LORD C. Nonsense! I am weary of this folly. Leave me.

DAVY. Yes, my Lord, I'm going. (*goes toward door; returning*) Did your lordship call?

LORD C. No. Begone.

DAVY. Yes. I am—I—(*goes to room L.H.; pushes open the door*) Lord, how dark it is. I beg your pardon, but you have not about you a morsel of candle?

LORD C. Away I tell you, the moon will shortly rise, and you will have light enough.

DAVY. I am going. (*in his absence of mind he takes up the candle*) Goodnight. (LORD C. *takes candle from him*) Exactly, I beg pardon—I—feel—I am going—good night.

ACT ONE : SCENE TWO

LORD C.   Good night, Davy, good night.

DAVY.   (*goes to room and returns*) I forgot to say—goodnight.

LORD C.   Will you leave me!

DAVY.   Yes my Lord, don't you see I am leaving you—I—ho! ho! (*sings*)

> 'Of all the birds that sang so sweet
> When of an eventide
> Upon the hawthorn bough they meet
> To carol side by side.'[29]

Song very loud as he enters the chamber L.H. Music. A pause. DAVY *is heard to utter a shout from chamber L.H.* LORD CLAVERING *starts up,* DAVY *runs in with his hair on end with terror, he falls on his knees and clutches* LORD CLAVERING'S *arm.*

LORD C.   How now?

DAVY.   There! There!

LORD C.   What? Speak!

DAVY.   Somebody—

LORD C.   Someone in yonder chamber? (DAVY *nods*) Impossible.

DAVY.   Someone on the ground I tell you. I was searching for a soft place to lie me down. I found what seemed to be a heap of clothes. Scarce had I settled myself to sleep upon it, when I found my pillow to be a human corse.[30]

LORD C.   If this alarm be but the creation of your brain I will cut your coward ears off. (*Takes candle and goes into chamber L.H.*)

DAVY.   I'll take to my heels while I have a whole skin. Here's a wedding night! (*Exit* DAVY *C.D.*)

LORD C.   (*Re-enter* LORD C *from L.H. pale and horror-stricken*) Horror! 'Tis true, a murderous deed has been recently done. Here lies young Roland Claire dead, a deep wound in his throat, but bloodless. And there he lay while we were feasting here, and she, too wretched girl, whose fears I derided, she sleeps there, while here her lover lies a corse. No, it must not be, she shall quit this fatal place. (*a prolonged cry heard within* Lucy's *room R.H.*) That cry! It is her voice! (*another cry*)

Lucy. (*within*) Help me, help!

Lord C. Perdition! She is not alone.

Throws down candle, it is extinguished. Stage dark. Enter Lucy *from her chamber R. Her hands clasp her neck as she reels forward.*

Lucy! Lucy!

Lucy. Help me! Murd—

Falls dead in the arms of Lord Clavering. Alan *enters from* Lucy's *room.*

Lord C. Murdered! Ha! A form steals from her chamber. (*draws pistol and fires at* Alan, *who utters a cry, and reeling forward falls across the table*)

Enter Ralph, Sir Guy, Nevil, Ellen, Maud, *and servants with lighted torches. Lights up.*

Lord C. Rookwood!

Alan. What have you done? I heard a cry for help, it came from a chamber next to that in which I slept. I burst the door of communication and entered only in time to see the murderer escape—he fled by that window. I hurried hither to obtain assistance when—ah!—

Lord C. I have murdered him.

Alan. Aye, I die by your hand.

Lord C. Forgive me, Sir. Oh! Forgive me. Let not your blood be upon my soul, for I am innocent of murder. (*kneels at his feet*)

Alan. Stand apart.

Lord C. Away!

Alan. On one condition I forgive thee—one.

Lord C. Name it.

ALAN. By the tenets of the religious sect, whose faith I rigidly profess, the dead must be consigned into the grave with an especial ceremony.

LORD C. I will perform it, speak.

ALAN. When I have breathed my last, let my body be conveyed amongst the peaks of Snowdon, and there exposed to the first rays of the rising moon which touch the earth.

LORD C. It shall be done. I swear it.

ALAN. Enough. I accept the oath.

ALAN dies. LORD CLAVERING *buries his face with his hands.*

SCENE THREE

Rocky pass in first grooves. Enter DAVY *R.H. At* LORD CLAVERING'*s exit, work calcium up*[31] *slowly, so as to touch the mountain top, and the body of* ALAN RABY. *Keep burning till curtain falls.*

DAVY. Oh! Lord, I have escaped from that horrible castle. I tumbled down stairs, scrambled over rocks, rolled over precipices, and here I am. Oh, here's a bridal night, here's mutual bliss. Oh! What would I give to be at home in bed—beside broomsticks with my head under the clothes. (*enter* NEVIL)

NEVIL. Who's there?

DAVY. (*falling on his knees*) Oh! He's after me I'm a dead man.

NEVIL. Arise you fool, and conduct us to the village.

DAVY. Eh, how you frightened me. I thought it was the devil.

NEVIL. Where is Lord Albert?

SIR GUY. We left him in the ruins. He said he would guard the body of the unfortunate Puritan till morning.

ELLEN. Oh, I'm sick with fright, let us on to the village, my heart is faint with terror.

NEVIL.   It has indeed been a night of terror to us all.

DAVY.   Look! (*points off R.H.*) See on yonder mountain path—see!

NEVIL.   It seems like the figure of a man struggling upward to the peaks of Snowdon.

RALPH.   He bears some dark burden in his arms.

DAVY.   'Tis Lord Albert, with the body of the Puritan.

ELLEN.   What can be his purpose?

SIR GUY.   To pitch him over into the chasm of the mountain.

DAVY.   No, the grave has never yet been dug deep enough to hold Alan Raby.

NEVIL.   This fellow is mad with fear. Come let us proceed to the village.

DAVY.   Follow me, the road is dangerous. One false step and you fall a thousand feet into an abyss.

SIR GUY.   The moon is rising and we soon shall have light enough.

DAVY.   This way.

Exeunt L.H. See LORD CLAVERING *and* ALAN *in place on the mountain before change.*

SCENE FOUR

The Peaks of Snowdon, no vegetation whatever is visible, but a sinister, tender bluish light gives a delicate character to the scene. On a ledge of rock, half scene high, LORD CLAVERING *is discovered with the body of* ALAN RABY *in his arms. Music. He lays over the body on the ledge of rock, and then descends a winding goat track.*

LORD C.   I have redeemed my oath. Oh! Let me hasten from this unearthly spot, this death-like solitude. (*exits R.H.*)

A pause. The moonlight is seen to tip the highest peak and creeps down the mountain. It arrives at the edge, and bathes the body of ALAN RABY *in a bright white light. After a moment, his chest begins to heave, his limbs to quiver, he raises his arm to his heart, and then, revived completely, rises to his full height.*

ALAN. (*addressing the moon*) Fountain of my life, once more thy rays restore me. Death—I defy thee!

END OF ACT ONE

Characters in Act Two

Alan Raby
Colonel Raby
Doctor Rees
Edgar Peveryl
Corporal Stump
Ada
Jenny

Act Two—Hall in Raby Castle

SCENE ONE

Scene: *Hall in Raby Castle, now restored. Time*: *1750.*

STUMP. (outside R. calling) Ho! Giles! Williams! Somebody! (enter STUMP with two valises)[1] So there is no one in the castle? A pretty watch is kept in this fort. Ho! Peter! Giles! (enter the servants) So you are awake at last, you rascals. (enter JENNY)

JENNY. What's all this riot? (*sees* STUMP) As I am a living woman, 'tis Johnnie Stump.

STUMP. Corporal. Full Corporal,[2] Jenny. But go quickly you fellows. (*to servants*) Colonel Raby and Captain Peveryl are impatient to get off their nags. Go take the horses to the stable, and arouse the household to meet the master. (*exit servants R.H.; cheers outside*) Ho! Already the servants have discovered our arrival, and see how they crowd around the Colonel.

JENNY. Let me crowd around you, Johnnie. Bless my heart what a splendid fellow you are.

STUMP. I am. It is useless to try and conceal it from your sex. Two years ago Johnnie went away to the wars in Flanders,[3] Johnnie was a lout, a bumpkin, a clod.[4] But two years' hard fighting have straightened the lout—he has left the skin of the bumpkin on a dozen glorious fields, and here comes Johnnie a' marching home again, another man. Are you the same girl I left behind me—let me see. (*kisses her*) Yes, pretty much.

JENNY. You did not leave that in the field of battle—I am afraid you have not been as faithful to your Jenny as she has been to you.

STUMP. Fidelity is—ahem—You see, fidelity is a creature of circumstance. It is a poor thing, Jenny, a very poor thing.

JENNY. So Giles Butler told me, when I would not be untrue to you.

STUMP. I'll break Giles Butler's head! Fidelity in a woman is a virtue, in a man it is a weakness. You see how I am improved. Your sex did it. Be grateful—you recollect what a ruin this castle of Raby was. It has passed through the hands of several owners, men of taste who rebuilt it, decorated it, and made it what it is. So it has been with me. I have passed through the hands of several owners of taste, who have made me what I am. They say a tailor makes the man, pooh! 'Tis a woman. Look at me and thank the former tenants. (*cheers renewed outside*)

Enter COLONEL RABY *and* EDGAR PEVERYL *with two servants.*

COL.   Thanks for your cheerful welcome. Go, some of you, and tell my daughter we have arrived, and the old doctor too, I hope he is well. Jenny, lass, bless your bright Welsh face. Every piece of furniture in these dear old halls of my forefathers seems to glow with pleasure on our return.

EDGAR.   'Tis strange that Ada is the last to greet us.

COL.   You forget, we have taken the castle by surprise. See, here comes your old tutor. (*enter* DOCTOR REES)

REES.   My dear Colonel and Edgar too. My kind friends, my dear boy. Glad I am to see you. Let me look at you.

COL.   He was a green boy when I took him from his studies. I bring him back a man, a true Peveryl. None the worse for the wound you heard of.

REES.   He was reported killed.

COL.   So I thought him, as I bore his body from the field. The surgeons gave him over. But thanks to the skill and sleepless care of a strange physician, your pupil was literally restored to life.

EDGAR.   We feared the news of my death might reach Raby Castle before you could hear of my recovery. So Rookwood undertook to convey the happier intelligence.

REES.   Leave us, Jenny, take your lover to the servants' hall.

COL.   Tell the butler to set a barrel of old ale abroach. The Corporal will be the hero of the kitchen. (*exeunt* JENNY *and* STUMP)

REES.   My friends, a strange and wild history has taken place in Raby Castle since your departure. When the news of Edgar's death arrived, our dearest child, your darling Ada, fell before it as a flower withered by lightning. A brain fever ensued, for five days I struggled with the fatal malady, but vainly. On the sixth day she awoke to consciousness, but only to breathe her last.

EDGAR.   Impossible, sir, she lives.

COL.   We have received letters from Rookwood, congratulating us upon her restoration to health.

REES.   She died, sir, died in these old arms. For a long week we watched beside her bier. The night before her funeral, a carriage drove into the castle yard, a stranger alighted, and I met him in this room. He came to see Ada. He said his name was Rookwood and delivered to me your letters. I told him they arrived too late, that she was dead. Still, he asked to see her. I would have refused but he waived me aside, and passed by me, finding his way into her chamber as if every avenue in the castle were familiar to him.

EDGAR.   Your story is strange.

REES.   We stood by her bedside; he gazed long upon her, and he then placed his hand upon her forehead; his brow contracted, his eyes seemed to glow with fire. Long time he stood thus, until I started with horror; a shudder quivered through the girl's form, she moved. The stranger smiled; he stooped down and pressed his lips to her brow, her eyes opened, and she drew a deep sigh.

COL.   She was in a trance.

REES.   Slowly, day-by-day, she recovered, but it is not the same life that lives in her; it seems not to be the same blood that flows in her veins. Her soul appears to cling to him for support; she obeys his gestures, and trembles beneath his gaze.

EDGAR.   In fact, my dear old Dominie,[5] Rookwood succeeded in a case where you had had failed; the army surgeons who condemned me declared that nothing but witchcraft could have restored my life.

REES.   Go to her Edgar, you will find her in the library. Heaven grant the sight of you may restore her spirit, and disenchant her soul!

COL.   Go, conduct her here.

EDGAR.   Love works wonders, sir. You will see what virtue there is in a kiss, what a spell lies within the circle of a lover's arms. (*exit*)

REES. I dared not tell him that she heard of his arrival without a sign of emotion, and when I would have conducted her to meet you, she burst into a flood of tears.

COL. What construction would you place on this strange condition? Has she ceased to love my nephew?

REES. No, but she loves as if she were dead. She remembers her past feeling, and speaks as a prisoner hopeless of release. Rookwood possesses a supernatural power over her. They commune together for hours in whispers, until she sinks into a profound and death-like sleep.

COL. You fill me with shapeless apprehensions. Give your fears some form. Of what do you suspect this man to whom we owe so much?

REES. I suspect him to be something more than human.

COL. Because he cured my child when you had given her up?

REES. No, because I have watched him, and he never eats, drinks, nor sleeps. At night he wanders from the castle into the mountains, and one bright moonlight night, from the high turret window, I followed his track with my telescope.

COL. For shame, Doctor, did you play the spy?

REES. He ascended to the very peak of Snowdon, and there upon a ledge of rock, he stood alone watching the moon rise. As the first rays fell over the snowy waste, he bared his breast and spread his arms towards the luminary.

COL. Perhaps he was only gathering herbs and simples, which some say must be culled at that hour to ensure their virtue.

REES. The next evening I climbed the mountain, and concealed myself near the spot. He came; again his breast seemed to drink in the moonbeams. I looked close, when I saw here, in his left bosom, just over the heart, an unclosed wound, as if a pistol bullet had passed through him!

COL. Ha! Ha! Would you have me believe this gentleman is dead as well as Ada? (*enter* ADA *and* EDGAR)

ADA. My dearest father. (*crosses C. and embraces* COLONEL RABY)

COL. My darling child, I do behold you again; but you look pale.

EDGAR.   She is still weak.

ADA.   No, your presence revives me; but forgive me, dear father, and you, Edgar, pardon me, if I am no longer the same thoughtless girl you once knew. I knew not how much I am changed until this moment, when I remember our parting, and I compare it now with our meeting.

EDGAR.   Her memory has faded; her hand fell listless into mine, and as I spoke words of love and fondness she echoed them, as from the hollowness of her heart.

ADA.   No! No, I love you more than ever, but I am still in the trance from which he recovered me.

EDGAR.   Your physician?

ADA.   Aye, and yours. Rookwood. When I fell into a trance, I saw you lying in your tent dead. I watched by your bedside during your recovery.

COL.   She raves!

ADA.   I saw Rookwood set forth to hasten hither, day and night he travelled. I saw the preparations for my funeral. Oh, it was a terrible thing, father, for I could not tell if they would bury me ere he arrived. I struggled to speak, to tell them he was coming, but I was cold and motionless, living, but dead.

COL.   This is indeed terrible, my child.

ADA.   But he came—he came, and he restored my life. It is his. When he approaches, a thrill quivers through my veins; I am enchanted by his eyes. I feel like a bird beneath the fascination of a serpent. But now he is absent from the castle, I breathe freely, I am myself, I am free.

EDGAR.   (*aside*) Oh, what a pang of suspicion is this that seizes my heart! Can it be that she loves him?

ADA.   Take me, Edgar, save me from his fatal influence. When I am yours I shall be free. Now I am his slave. Take me to the shelter of your arms!

COL.   My dearest, Ada, all this is only the effect of an overwrought imagination; as your strength returns you will laugh at these follies. (*music*)

ADA. No, it is not folly, for now—now—I feel that he is approaching this room. He crosses the battlements—see, he enters the corridor—his eyes are fixed upon me.

EDGAR. (*gazing at her*) You cannot see him.

ADA. But my soul can.

COL. Ada!

ADA. He comes! He comes! (*enter* ALAN RABY *C. from L.*)

COL. Rookwood!

EDGAR. 'Tis he!

ALAN. Behold your child, Colonel Raby, restored to life.

EDGAR. She trembles. Lean upon me, dearest, let me lead you forth into the air. We will revisit the spots so dear to us both, and where as children we exchanged our love.

ADA. I cannot!

ALAN. Go, Ada; go.

ADA. Come. (*exit* ADA *and* EDGAR *C.R.*)

COL. (*crossing R.C.*) Doctor, I see that the corporal has arrived with our luggage. You will find amongst it a box marked with your name; it contains some choice volumes, a rare feast for you. I found them in Flanders. They contain some works on your favorite themes, witchcraft and necromancy;[6] there is also a collection of monkish recipes, and a book of Arabian charms.

REES. (*To* COLONEL RABY) If I could only find amongst them a recipe to exorcise the devil.

COL. Hush! (*Exit* DOCTOR REES)

ALAN. You are surprised, Colonel Raby, to account wherefore one who is a stranger to you and yours should bestow obligations on your family, which you know not how to repay.

COL. My very thoughts.

ACT TWO : SCENE ONE

ALAN. Is my name unknown to the records of your family?

COL. Rookwood! Rookwood! I have heard the name connected with ours.

ALAN. Gervase Rookwood.

COL. Ah, I remember now. A Puritan officer of that name was killed in this very castle by misadventure some hundred years ago, and by my faith, it was in this very room the deed was done.

ALAN. Amongst the papers left by that Rookwood, this document was lately discovered. (*Hands a paper to* COLONEL RABY) It is the will of Alan Raby. It bequeaths this castle and estates to his brother in arms, Gervase Rookwood, my ancestor.

COL. (*perusing the deed*) Impossible, yet this deed appears to be in Alan Raby's own handwriting. If this be so, you claim to be master of the acres I usurp, and Lord of Raby Castle!

ALAN. Such was my object in seeking you, but your fair daughter has inspired me with another purpose. Bestow her beauteous person upon me in lieu of the estate; you owe her life to me. You will but pay a debt.

COL. Her troth and my word are pledged to her cousin Edgar.

ALAN. He will release her from the bond when he finds it no longer binds her heart.

COL. Does Ada know of this claim?

ALAN. You suspect she would sacrifice her young life to me to preserve your future. I needed no such means to win her love.

COL. This news will break my poor Edgar's heart. (*re-enter* EDGAR)

EDGAR. I have learned the truth, sir. I have drawn it from her. She loves him. She has confessed to me the terrible fascination he possesses over her. She clung to me with tears, and madly repeated her vows to me, but I knew they came not from her heart. (*to* ALAN) You saved my life, but you have robbed me of all that made life dear. (*enter* ADA)

ADA. Edgar, dear Edgar—Oh, do not leave me.

COL. Listen, my child. There stands your lover, here the savior of your dear life; both love you. Let your heart judge between these two men.

ADA. My father. My father. (*stands bewildered*)

COL. I will leave you to decide. (*exit R.1.E.*)

ADA. What do I hear?

ALAN. You hear that I love you. Ada, my soul, are you not mine; are you not she whom I have snatched from the jaws of death? I love you; your young life shall revive me, and for this end I bade you live.

ADA. What power is this that oppresses me?

ALAN. It is my will; mine eyes are fixed upon thy heart as if with fangs. While my soul like a serpent entwines thine within its folds and crushes thee to my will. Ada, thou art mine.

ADA. Spare me. Yes, thou art my master; I cannot oppose thee.

EDGAR. (*going to* ADA) She turns away from me, not one look. Ada, Ada, will you not speak to me? Will you part thus from me?

ADA. Edgar, no, no—I love you—my heart is—

ALAN. Peace!

EDGAR. Farewell! I would that I could have made you happy. (*going*)

ADA. Do not leave me.

EDGAR. I cannot bear to witness your love bestowed upon another. Farewell, dearest Ada, may you be happy. (*exit C.D.*)

ADA. Edgar! Edgar! (*going*)

ALAN. Stay! Retire to your chamber, and remain there until my will beckons thee to come.

ADA. I obey. (*exit* ADA *R.2.E.*)

ALAN. She is mine! A new life drawn from the pure heart of a maiden of my race and blood must enter this form. Ada shall be the victim. Her life for mine.

SCENE TWO

A room in the castle. Enter DOCTOR REES *with a large volume, followed by* STUMP, *bearing a pile of books.* JENNY *follows them.*

REES. What a mine of wealth the Colonel has brought me. What a precious store.

JENNY. They smell awful musty; shall I dust 'em, Doctor?

REES. Dust 'em! I'll dust you if you so much as blow a speck off. (*reads*) *Principia Demonia* by Duns Scotus,[7] being a compendium of the Black Craft[8] containing a full and true account of authenticated evil spirits inhabiting human form. Ghouls, Djinns, Bogles, Vampires.[9] (*he reads apart*)

JENNY. I hope I have not got any evil spirits in my apron. What's this? (*looking at a book*) 'Christian advice to young people about to marry'.[10] I don't want anybody's advice, do you, Johnnie?

STUMP. What does it say? It might put us up to something.

JENNY. (*reading*) Chapter One: The duties of a wife.

REES. The devil prefers the female form, and evil spirits more frequently inhabit that sex.

JENNY. (*shutting the book*) I don't believe a word of it. Here is half a volume about a matter that could be put into three lines.

STUMP. Do you know the duties of a wife?

JENNY. By heart! They are not learned in a book. She is always up first, makes the fire, cleans up and gets breakfast, washes everything, cooks the dinner, tidies around, waits up for you at night while you are drinking at a public house, creeps out after you, and leads you home drunk, puts you to bed, and swears to all the neighbors that you are the best of husbands.

STUMP. Jenny, your ideas of matrimony coincide with mine exactly.

REES. Oh! Powers of darkness, what's this? (STUMP *crosses to R. of* REES) 'The vampire: this strange monster is well authenticated. Chiefly known in Germany,[11] it is said if a dead person be exposed to the light of the first rays of the rising moon which touch the earth, a false life is instilled into the corpse'.

STUMP. Oh, Lord!

REES. (*reading*) 'Which possesses movement, and all signs of ordinary existence, except that there is no pulsation in the heart. This creature living against the will of heaven, eats not, drinks not, nor does he require the refreshment of sleep'. I am all over a cold perspiration.

STUMP. What does he live on?

REES. 'This Phantom recruits its life by drawing the life blood from the veins of the living, but more especially it chooses victims from amongst maidens of his own race and blood, pure and spotless. As the body of this monster is bloodless, so his face is said to be as pale as death'.

JENNY. Oh, dear! The old Dominie is going to faint.

REES. Jenny. Johnnie. Let me recover my reason. Is there not a legend in the village, a terrible story about this castle?

JENNY. The curse of Raby.

REES. At long intervals the Phantom of Alan Raby visits this place, and his presence is known by the mysterious death of some daughter of his race.

STUMP. Fifty years ago, the beautiful Maud Raby was found murdered on the south battlement, the night before her bridal.

JENNY. And it was said she was a victim of the curse of Raby. (*enter* EDGAR)

EDGAR. Go Corporal, the Colonel wants you.

STUMP. Come along, Jenny. (*crosses to R.H.*)

JENNY. How pale Mister Edgar looks, something is wrong upstairs in the parlor,[12] Johnnie; that black doctor is at the bottom of it. (*exeunt* STUMP *and* JENNY)

REES. Edgar, my boy, what is the matter?

EDGAR. My dear tutor, Ada loves me not, and I have fled from the sight of that happiness, which she has bestowed upon another.

REES. Another!

EDGAR. You see this deed? (*showing a will*) It is the will of Sir Alan Raby.

REES. (*examines the paper*) Conveyance of the lands of Raby to Gervase Rookwood. Surely I am not in my senses. How came this deed in your possession?

EDGAR. This stranger is here to prefer his claim. My uncle admits it, already he has summoned the tenants to attend in the great hall, that he may present to them their new Lord.

REES. You are all mad together. What, render up this castle and estate to this charlatan[13]—beggar his child?

EDGAR. No, for Ada loves her preserver and consents to bestow on him her hand in marriage.

REES. Wedded to him! And to save his property the Colonel consents?

EDGAR. You wrong him, Doctor, indeed you do, and how can I reproach Rookwood? Who could help loving my darling one? Oh, why did I survive my wound; was I brought back to life for this? (*crosses up to R.H.*)

REES. The deed seems to be genuine! Yet if so, why has the claim remained dormant for a hundred years?

EDGAR. The document has only been discovered lately.

REES. This is indeed the hand of Alan Raby; there are many of his old papers in the family chest, in the same singular, unmistakable writing. Yet this ink has not faded, and turned yellow. Some quality of the paper may have preserved it. (*looking intently at paper*)

EDGAR. Why search so idly, and so curiously?

REES. Ha! I knew it, ah! Double imposter, have I caught you. Je triumphe![14] Quae![15] Shout you dog! Jump you rascal, Eureka![16] I have discovered him! Unmask him!

EDGAR. Are you mad?

REES. You shall judge—What is the date of this deed, see?

EDGAR. (*reading*) Done on the 9th day of August 1654.

REES. Now look for the watermark upon the paper, can you distinguish it?

EDGAR. (*reading*) 1750. What does this mean?

REES.   The writing is in Alan Raby's hand, written by him, on paper manufactured one hundred years after his death.

EDGAR.   'Tis a forgery!

REES.   Hush! It is no forgery. Were I to tell you my suspicions about this stranger, you would laugh at my fears. But here is proof enough, to defeat his horrid purpose, and save Ada from his clutch. The Colonel will never bestow his daughter on an imposter. (*shouts outside*) Hark, the tenants are assembling. Take the deed and rescue the child. Why do you pause?

EDGAR.   I had rather face a platoon of infantry,[17] and charge unarmed upon their front, than face this man, with such a weapon as this in my hand, and strike him speechless to my foot, helpless with shame. (*exit L.1.E.*)

REES.   He will not fall without a struggle. Let us be prepared for the worst. What say my Duns Scotus? Where's my compendium? What says *Principia*? (*reads*) 'The vampire can be destroyed by fire or by a wound which must pierce his heart. After death, let the body be kept from the moonlight, for the virtue of its rays will revive the monster.' I shall not feel the smallest compunction in administering that prescription if circumstances require the dose. (*exit R.1.E. Music*)

SCENE THREE

A room in the castle. Table R.H. with books and writing materials upon it. ALAN RABY, COLONEL RABY, JENNY, CORPORAL STUMP, *and peasants discovered. Also* ADA RABY.

COL.   Has my nephew been summoned? His presence is necessary to this act of justice.

STUMP.   The Captain is here. (*looking off C. Enter* EDGAR *very pale*)

COL.   Where is the Doctor?

EDGAR.   His presence is needless, sir. I understand your purpose is to admit the claim of this person to the Lordship of Raby, and you have called the tenantry to witness your cession of the estate.

COL.   To its rightful owner.

EDGAR.   He declines to accept it.

ACT TWO : SCENE THREE

COL.   Are you in your senses, Edgar?

EDGAR.   Perfectly. I repeat the words: he declines to accept it.

COL.   Explain yourself.

EDGAR.   I will do so, to him alone. Leave us together, sir, the few words I have to speak will convince him he has no claim beyond our gratitude for the lives he has preserved. (JENNY *crosses to* ADA *who rises*)

COL.   This is a strange demand, and seems to cover some mystery.

EDGAR.   It does so, sir. (*crosses to R.H.* STUMP *crosses up C.*)

COL.   Come, Ada. (*he conducts her to R.3.E. then all retire but* ALAN *and* EDGAR)

EDGAR.   Begone! And take with you this proof of your imposture, you are discovered. This deed has been lately executed. I spare your life, forfeit by this forgery. You saved mine, we are quits.

ALAN.   And you hope to efface my image in Ada's heart by this discovery? Fool, she loves me, and the news will kill her.

EDGAR.   Then meet me tonight—at once—with what weapon you choose, and let the survivor of a deadly combat claim her hand.

ALAN.   Agreed! In an hour hence the moon will rise and afford us light enough for what we have to do.

EDGAR.   The place?

ALAN.   There is a ledge of rock on the eastern summit of Snowdon; it overhangs the torrent.

EDGAR.   You select a strange place.

ALAN.   He that falls may be left there, and need no burial; no human being visits that rugged solitude.

EDGAR.   In an hour hence, I will meet you there. (*exit* EDGAR *C.*)

ALAN.   In an hour. 'Tis not his blood can revive my failing life, 'tis Ada's lovely spirit must pass into my heart and—now—now—she cannot escape me. Where is she? I see her—she sleeps fitfully, she is alone with the village girl. Ada! Ada! Bid her begone, I would be alone with thee. So—'tis well.

Enter JENNY *from room R.H. She crosses and passes out C.D.*

Now, arise—she obeys me. Come hither—I command thee. She obeys me—she is a slave to my will. (*enter* ADA *R.H.*) She sleeps.

ADA.   I am here.

ALAN.   Ada. (*she recoils from his touch*)

ADA.   Oh, let me sleep.

ALAN.   No, awake, and be thyself; thy hour has come.

ADA.   Oh, my brain reels.

ALAN.   Thou knowest me?

ADA.   From what horrible dream do I awake?

ALAN.   Ada.

ADA.   Oh, you here? Leave me, release me from this fearful bondage. I cannot resist the power that oppresses me—Oh, touch me not—thy touch strikes cold into my heart. Spare me!

ALAN.   Why do you look so upon one who loves you?

ADA.   Because you inspire me with fear.

ALAN.   'Tis love, not fear. Thy soul is mine. Come to my breast, see thou can'st not escape the spell my spirit has cast on thine.

ADA.   No, No, 'tis not love, it cannot be. I cannot love thee.

ALAN.   You cannot?

ADA.   Because the heart whereon you press me seemed to be the bosom of a corpse, and from the heart within I feel no throb of life.

ALAN.   Ah! Thou knowest me, I am thy doom. Ada, the curse of Raby is in the Castle Hall, and claims thy forfeit life.

ACT TWO : SCENE THREE

ADA. Away, Phantom! Demon! My father, help! Edgar! Ah, my voice is choked with fear. Avoid thee, fiend, abhorrent spectre! (*she retreats before him into her room R.H.*)

ALAN. Thy hour has come. (*enter* REES *from* ADA's *room*)

REES. Not yet!

ALAN. Perdition! What means this folly?

REES. It means that I have doubt in my mind whether Duns Scotus is a reliable authority, and I have given you the benefit of that doubt. Begone at once! Put the broad seas between you and me ere daylight. Take my advice, if you don't I'll take his pistol and put a bullet in your cold heart.

ALAN. (*aside*) Edgar awaits me, least for him there is no escape. At one blow I can satisfy my hate, wreak my revenge, and revive my drooping life. (*exits*)

REES. Lord, I am all over a perspiration. Jenny! Stump! Come quickly. (*enter* JENNY *and* STUMP) Go to your mistress, she has fainted. Do not leave her side on any pretense until we return. (*exit* JENNY *into room R.H.*) Now, Corporal, where are the Colonel's pistols?

STUMP. In his bed chamber.

REES. Go fetch them, and tell him to come here at once, and remain with Ada. You must go with me.

STUMP. Where?

REES. I don't mean to lose sight of Rookwood until I see him safely out of this country. Have you a good shot?

STUMP. The crack of my corps. Throw up a guinea and I'll bring down a wedding ring.

REES. Are the Colonel's pistols true?

STUMP. As gospel.

REES. Then follow me, for I may want them to preach. (*exeunt L.1.E.*)

SCENE FOUR

The peaks of Snowdon. EDGAR *discovered on mountain.*

EDGAR. How chill the air is on this height, but how pure. The slightest sound is audible. Hark! A footstep. Yes, a dark form emerges from yonder group of rocks, 'tis Rookwood! (*enter* ALAN *L.H.*)

ALAN. I am here.

EDGAR. Our business needs no preface, sir. I am at your service.

ALAN. Yonder is the rock; follow me.

Exeunt and re-enter upon the ledge of rocks. They take off their coats and waistcoats.

EDGAR. Now, sir, I am ready, but there is scarce room enough to engage our weapons—they are too long.

ALAN. But this is short enough. (*casts himself on Edgar with a poignard*)[18]

EDGAR. A dagger! Ah, traitor! Murderer!

EDGAR *falls.* ALAN *kneels over him.*

ALAN. Take it in thy throat, let me slake my thirst in thy life blood.

A shot is heard outside. ALAN *falls back with a cry.* EDGAR *rises. Enter* DOCTOR REES *and* CORPORAL STUMP *L.H.*

STUMP. I say, Doctor, I rung the bell, didn't I?

EDGAR. Doctor! Corporal—from what a monster have you preserved me! (*disappears from ledge*)

REES. See a party with torches ascend; it is the Colonel. (*enter* COLONEL RABY, ADA, *and* JENNY *L.H.*)

COL. I heard the sound of fire-arms.

ADA. Where is Edgar? (*enter* EDGAR *R.H.*)

EDGAR. Here, dearest Ada, here, my own! (*embraces* ADA, REES *exits R.H.*)

ACT TWO : SCENE THREE

ADA. Dear, dear, Edgar, the fearful influence of that man has passed from me, and I am your own again.

EDGAR. Yonder lies the body of the wretch who would have taken my life by treachery. Who fired that shot?

STUMP. The Doctor gave the word and I sent the message.

COL. But come, let us return home, the moon is rising it will light our path. Let us hasten to the castle. Tomorrow the body of that wretch may be removed. Let it lie there 'till we can send assistance from the village.

EDGAR. Where is my preserver, where is the Doctor? (DOCTOR REES *appears on the ledge of rocks*)

REES. Here I am, don't be anxious. I have a little duty to perform up here. I shan't be long.

EDGAR. What can he mean?

REES. Aye, now, for the prescription. (*reads from book*) 'It is said if the dead body of the vampire be exposed to the first rays of the rising moon, which touch the earth, a false life is instilled into the corpse'. And, see, he revives! He revives!

COL. Stop, Doctor, I command you!

REES. (*reads*) 'After death, his body must be kept from the moonlight, lest by virtue of its rays he might revive'. See, watch his heaving form, already the life comes back to him limb by limb.

COL. Hold! What would you do?

REES. Exterminate the Phantom. Into this black chasm, where the light of heaven never visited I cast his body. May his dark spirit sink as low into eternal perdition!

Casts the body over the chasm. When DOCTOR REES *hurls the body of* ALAN RABY *over the ledge of rocks, the characters stand on the picture. Slow Curtain.*

THE END

Emendation List

———•◆•◆•———

THE FOLLOWING LIST INCLUDES all the emendations made to the copy texts to produce this volume's texts of *The Vampire* and *The Phantom*. The copy text for *The Vampire* is a holograph manuscript in Dion Boucicault's hand, dated 1852 (MS-V); that for *The Phantom* is a handwritten prompt book in a copyist's hand with emendations by Boucicault, prepared in 1873 (PB-P). Emendations have been made where the source material clearly does not reflect the author's intentions: in other words, where later decisions to MS-V and PB-P were not applied and clearly do not follow the logic of the texts. Quotations from manuscript materials in the present volume are generally reading transcriptions, but where references to corrections are necessary here deletions are represented <thus> and insertions ^thus^.

Errors in the spelling of proper nouns have been emended, but accepted variants in the spelling of place names are retained, to accurately reflect the copy text. The spellings used in *The Phantom* observe American English orthographic conventions employed in the copy text. Except where noted, errors in quotations have been left uncorrected in the text, as this reflects the fluidity of intertextual citation employed by authors like Dion Boucicault during the nineteenth century. Simple repair work (a missing hyphen at the end of a line, missing full-stop at the end of a sentence, the lack of one of a pair of quotation marks or parentheses, and so on) has been silently implemented and is not noted in the list below. Stage directions, likewise, have been standardized and made consistent with each other and the list of Abbreviated Stage Directions supplied in the Note on the Texts, p. xxx. Inconsistent use of italicization, particularly for names and places, capitalization and hyphenation have not been regularized to a 'house style', but instead follows preponderant usage within the copy text as a guide. Where this has not been possible, emendations have been guided by consulting examples of contemporary usage in the *Oxford English Dictionary*. Where such corrections are made, these have been indicated below. For more details about general emendations that have been implemented and the Gothic Originals house style, please consult the Note on the Text (pp. xxviii–xxx).

In the following lists, the reading of the present text is given first, by page and line number, followed by the source of the new reading, and then after a square bracket, the original reading of the copy text and (if necessary) the reasoning behind the emendation. Line numbering counts chapter titles, chapter decorations and subtitles, but not blank lines.

EMENDATION LIST

THE VAMPIRE

Abbreviations for witnesses used in the following emendations are as follows:

MS-V   79pp. holograph MS in Boucicault's hand, written in April 1852, and missing Act III, Scene 3 (this edition's copy text)

LC-V   63pp. handwritten script submitted to the Lord Chamberlain's Office, licensed on 25 May 1852 for presentation at the Royal Princess's Theatre in London

PB-V   handwritten prompt book prepared for James Wallack of New York by Boucicault's prompter, T. H. Edmonds, in 1852

5.7–8   *Watkyn Rees* (LC-V, PB-V)] *Davy Rees*
MS-V has 'Davy' throughout Act I. 'Davy' is struck out with 'Watkyn' above; both LC-V and PB-V have 'Watkyn' exclusively.

5.20   king (MS-V)] <tyrant>
MS-V originally refers to Cromwell as a 'tyrant', and deletes the following line from WATKYN: 'Ay, a savage is better off than a tenant'.

6.14   Tremadoc (LC-V, PB-V)] Wrexham
Tremadoc [Tremadog], which is 60 miles (96 km) west of Wrexham (Wrecsam), a town in NW Wales.

8.26   Llanberis (LC-V, PB-V)] Llanfair
Llanfair (Welsh for 'Church of St Mary') most likely refers to the village in Gwynedd on the NW coast of Wales, some 5 miles (8 km) south of Tremadog.

12.16–17   ^*In the distance is seen the clock tower.*^ (PB-V)
21.10   ^(*raises himself from table*)^ (PB-V)
21.23   ^into the grave^ (PB-V)
22.16   *Curtain descends.*
PB-V notes that Act I ran for 35 minutes.

27.7–13   ^TREV. You were always a perfection. ... (*a distant shout is heard*)^ (LC-V, PB-V)
These lines are crossed out in MS-V, but included in both LC-V and PB-V.

28.10–11   ^(*shaking hands heartily with him and putting her face up to him*)^ (PB-V)

38.28   *Act drop.*
PB-V notes that Act II ran for 28 minutes.

56.1–57.9   ^SCENE FOUR ... *Curtain.*^ (LC-V)
The entire final scene is missing from MS-V: LC-V was utilized for this section.

EMENDATION LIST

THE PHANTOM

Abbreviations for witnesses used in the following emendations are as follows:

MS-P   133pp. holograph prompt book in two parts, alternating between Boucicault's hand and an unknown copyist, watermarked 1852

HD-P   incomplete 14pp. holograph draft in Boucicault's hand, amending Act II, watermarked 1852

RC-P   49pp. handwritten rehearsal copy (heavily prompted), amending Act II, watermarked 1852

PB-P   113-pp. handwritten prompt book in a copyist's hand, containing emendations by Boucicault, undated but used for 1873 performance (this edition's copy text)

61.4–22   *Enter Janet ... Ay, every dog has his day.* (PB-P)
Here, PB-P substitutes the explanatory historical information as given here, confirming the action takes place during the English Civil War, for humorous dialogue published in the 1856 Samuel French version, which reads as follows (p. 3):

    Davy. [*Off at door as he enters.*] Good-bye, neighbors, good-bye.

    Janet. So, Davy, we are married.

    Davy. Yes, I'm a bride—a blushing bride—I confess I feel a little nervous; you have been married before—it is no novelty to you.

    Janet. Don't fear, Davy, you'll make an excellent husband—you have only one fault.

    Davy. I am a coward; I could not bear to be alone in the dark, but you pointed out a remedy I never should have thought of. 'Davy,' says you, 'marry me and you'll never be alone in the dark again.'

    Janet. Be off with you to the stable, lock up all round, and then we will spend our wedding evening like a pair of pigeons.

    Davy. [*Aside.*] I don't know how it is. but I feel a little nervous.
                                                       [*A distant peal of thunder*

    Janet. Hark! a storm is coming down the mountain—make haste back. Oh, Davy, there is nothing so delightful as making love under cosy shelter in a thunder storm.

    Davy. Listen. I hear the clatter of a horse's hoofs—it can't be a customer.

73.24–25   Here's a wedding night!
While Boucicault excised most of the references to Davy and Jenny's impending nuptials, it appears this line was missed in PB-P, or main-

EMENDATION LIST

	tained to refer to the promised fifty guineas and Jenny's hinted desire to marry a wealthier Davy.
86.6	for this <cruel> end (PB-P)
95.7	castle. Tomorrow] castle, tomorrow

Explanatory Notes

THE FOLLOWING NOTES ATTEMPT TO IDENTIFY Boucicault's sources, quotations, proverbial phrases and references to historical events and personages, as well as geographical locations and obscure or specialist language. Reference is by superscript arabic numerals that restart at each significant section of the volume, notably the two play texts and the fresh acts. In general, only the first occurence of a specific term is glossed, given the sequential nature of the texts, but terms occurring in both *The Vampire* and *The Phantom* are glossed fresh at initial apperance for each text. Cross-references to other notes refer to Act (in roman small caps) and the note number (following a comma, and prefixed by 'n.'). References to the Bible are taken from the Authorized Version, while the abbreviation *OED* indicates defintions that have been taken from the most recent edition of the *Oxford English Dictionary*, available online at *https://www.oed.com*.

THE VAMPIRE

Half-title
1. *Phantasm:* 'A thing or being which apparently exists but is not real; a hallucination or vision; a figment of the imagination; an illusion.' (*OED*)

The First Drama—Raby Castle [Act I]
1. *Raby Peveryl:* Neither 'Raby' nor 'Peveryl' are Welsh placenames, but connect more closely to two Norman-era landholdings in the English Midlands and North.

    A historic Raby Castle, dating back to the 13th century, is to be found near Staindrop, Co. Durham, NE England. The feudal barony of Raby dates back to the time of Geoffrey de Neville, 1st Baron of Neville of Raby (d. c. 1242).

    A ruin by the late 16th century, Peveril Castle overlooks the village of Castleton in Derbyshire, and was built at least as early as 1086. It was named for William Peverel (d. 1114), a favourite, and reputedly the natural son, of William the Conqueror. The name 'Peverel' allegedly derives from the Latin *puerulus* (small boy) or *piper* (pepper), according to J. R. Planché's *The Conqueror and his Companions*, 2 vols (London: Tinsley Brothers, 1874), II, 258–75. The name and castle famously feature in the title of Sir Walter Scott's longest novel, *Peveril of the Peak* (1823), which is set during the Restoration period, with most of the action taking place in 1678.
2. *fete:* 'An entertainment on a large scale; a festival, a celebration' *(OED)*, from the Anglo–Norman *fette*, a feast.
3. *mead:* alcoholic beverage made from fermenting honey and water.

4. *roundhead:* supporter of the Parliamentary faction during the English Civil War (1642–1651), who favoured constitutional over absolute monarchy. 'Roundhead' was originally a pejorative term, applied to the Parliamentarians because many of them wore their hair cropped close. They were opposed by the Royalist faction titled Cavaliers (see I, n. 14, below). During the mid-17th century, Wales was divided by the Roundhead and Cavalier factions.
5. *Cromwell:* Oliver Cromwell (1599–1658) was a politician and soldier, who led the Parliamentary faction during the English Civil War. Following the execution of King Charles I (for which he advocated) in January 1649, Cromwell governed as Lord Protector of the Commonwealth until his death in 1658.
6. *Snowdon:* Set within Snowdonia, North Wales, Snowdon (*Yr Wyddfa* in Welsh) is the tallest mountain in Wales and the highest in the British Isles below the Scottish highlands, standing at 3560 ft (1085 m).
7. *roebuck:* male of the roe deer (*Capreolus*).
8. *Puritan:* member of the austere English Protestant sect from the late 16th and 17th centuries, who sought to complete the reformation of the Anglican Church to remove any crypto-Catholic elements of church practice, which they considered corrupt or unscriptural. The Puritans were associated strongly with the Parliamentary faction during the English Civil War.
9. *the fiend:* the Devil.
10. *he is dead:* This is incorrect: in fact, Cromwell had died on 3 September 1658, nearly two years prior to the events of Act I.
11. *King Charles restored:* Charles II (1630–1685), son of Charles I, was restored to the thrones of England, Scotland and Ireland on 29 May 1650 and ruled until his death. Charles II belonged to the House of Stuart.
12. *Charles the First:* Born in 1600, Charles I was the son of James VI of Scotland and I of England (1566–1625), whom he succeeded as the second Stuart King of England, Scotland and Ireland from 1625 until his execution by beheading in 1649, during the English Civil War (1642–1651).
13. *Tremadoc:* anglicized version of the Welsh *Tremadog*, a village in the county of Gwynedd, NW Wales, 10 miles (16 km) south of Snowdon.
14. *cavaliers:* supporters of the Royalist faction during the English Civil War (1642–1651), who favoured absolute monarchy and supported the cause of the Stuart monarchs (see I, nn. 11–12, above). The term, derived from the French *chevalier* (horseman), was used pejoratively by their opponents in the Parliamentary faction, known as Roundheads (see I, n. 4, above).
15. *newly recovered estates:* Following the Restoration of Charles II in 1649, loyal members of the Royalist cause regained properties and lands which had been previously sequestered by the Parliamentarians.
16. *Welsh frontier:* borderlands separating England and Wales.
17. *Milford:* town on the outskirts of Newton, Powys in mid-Wales, approximately 80 miles (130 km) SE of Snowdon. Not to be confused with Milford Haven, in Pembrokeshire, SW Wales, which is some 150 miles (240 km) south of Snowdon.
18. *goblins:* small, ugly creatures of folk and fairy tales, considered as malevolent or merely mischievous (*OED*).
19. *Ralph ap Gwynne:* The Welsh 'ap' is a patronymic, although in this case it links Norman and Welsh names—'Ralph, son of Gwyn'.

20. *Llanberis:* village in Gwynedd, NW Wales, at the foot of Snowdon (see I, n. 6, above); the name is Welsh for 'The Church of St Peris', an early Christian saint, possibly from the 6th century.
21. *Mill gap:* most likely, the Llanberis Pass, which lies between the Snowdon and Glyderau massifs.
22. *Naseby:* The defeat of the Royalist forces by Cromwell's troops just outside the village of Naseby in Northamptonshire on 14 June 1645 was pivotal in the English Civil War, leading to the eventual defeat of the forces of Charles I. After the Battle of Naseby, and up to the surrender by the Royalists besieged in Oxford in June 1646, the war was essentially a 'mopping up operation'—see J. C. Davis, *Oliver Cromwell* (London: Arnold, 2001), p. 95
23. *Ireton:* Henry Ireton (c. 1611–1651), an English general in the Parliamentary army, and Cromwell's son-in-law. His troops were broken by a charge led by Prince Rupert, cousin of Charles II, leading to Ireton's wounding and brief capture.

    dragoon: the term was originally applied to mounted infantrymen armed with the dragoon musket (so called for its 'firebreathing' associations), after whom they were named. 'These gradually developed into horse soldiers, and the term is now merely a name for certain regiments of cavalry which historically represent the ancient dragoons, and retain some distinctive features of dress, etc.' (*OED*).
24. *myrmidons:* members of a bodyguard or retinue; faithful followers (*OED*).
25. *your wig is getting out of curl:* Boucicault is likely referring to the trend of men's wigs made popular by Charles II after his restoration to the throne. These 'periwigs' were often worn over shaved heads and had irregular curls framing the face and spreading below the shoulders—see C. Willett Cunnington and Phillis Cunnington, *Handbook of English Costume in the Seventeenth Century* (Boston: PLAYS, Inc., 1972), p. 164.
26. *abominable bat:* The bat here is likely coincidence, but, as Sharon Gallagher notes, the tie to vampire mythology is notable—see *The Irish Vampire* (Jefferson, NC: McFarland & Co., 2017), p. 85.
27. *pledge:* to drink with or to a person as a gesture of goodwill; archaic (*OED*).
28. *burgundy:* wine from the Burgundy region of eastern France, typically dry reds made from pinot noir grapes or whites from chardonnay grapes.
29. *musquetoon:* also, 'musketoon', '[a] kind of musket with a short barrel and a large bore' (*OED*).
30. *Holstein:* region of northern Germany between the Elbe and Eider rivers.
31. *St. George:* George of Lydda (d. 303), Christian martyr and venerated saint of Cappadocian Greek origin; patron saint of a number of countries, including England.
32. *the Demon:* the Devil.
33. *puritan garb:* The austere Puritans were associated with equally plain and moderst clothing, favouring dark- or drab-coloured clothing made from wool or linen. The popular image of Puritans wearing black was an exaggeration or misattribution, given the expense of black dye: black clothing was thus reserved for special occasions or favoured by wealthy Puritans.
34. *horn of wine:* hollowed animal horn used as a drinking vessel.
35. *fratricide:* someone who has killed one's brother(s).

36. *Of all the birds ... side by side:* untraced; likely a creation of Boucicault.
37. *corse:* corpse.
38. *forte:* 'A musical direction indicating a strong, loud tone in performance' (*OED*).

The Second Drama—Raby Hall [Act II]
1. *chandelier:* ornamental lighting fitting, typically made up of branches that carry multiple lights, and made to be hung from the ceiling.
2. *Peveryl:* For a discussion of the origins and associations of the Peveril/Peveryl name, see I, n. 1, above.
3. *George III:* King of Great Britain and Ireland from 1760 until his death in 1820.
4. *soirée:* social gathering that occurred in the evening, and consisting of refreshments and interesting or convival conversation.
5. *hunt the slipper:* party game, in which participants must locate an object hidden by one of their fellows, the winner being the first to locate it.
6. *ombre:* from the Spanish *ombre*, 'man'; a fast-paced card game, based on taking tricks and gaining popularity across Europe from the 17th century onwards.

    piquet: another trick-taking card game that originated in 16th-century France, rather than Spain, although it may be ultimately of Spanish origin as well.
7. *minuet:* social dance for two people, originating in France and popular from the early 18th century onward.
8. *Florence:* city in central Italy (Italian *Firenze*) and capital of the Tuscany region; a centre of medieval trade and viewed as the birthplace of the Renaissance. As the language of Dante, Boccaccio and Petrarch, the Florentine dialect formed the basis of modern Italian.
9. *Edgar and Emma:* 'Edgar' and 'Emma' were stereotypical names associated with sentimental romance during the late 18th century, and would have signalled unparalleled devotion between the lovers. In her juvenilia, Jane Austen satirized sentimental fiction, which was popular during her youth, by writing a short novel titled 'Edgar and Emma', which comprised a handful of pages.
10. *1st July Old Style 1760:* The Julian Calendar was a dating style used until 1752, with the year beginning on March 25th. It was replaced by the Gregorian Calendar, with the year beginning on January 1st. The Julian Calendar was referred to as 'Old Style Dating', in contrast to the 'New Style Dating' of the Gregorian system.
11. *droll:* unintentionally amusing.
12. *Venus:* Roman goddess of love, who equated to the ancient Greek deity Aphrodite.
13. *hoop:* 18th-century fashion popularized the use of hoop underskirts or petticoats, which used whalebone, cane, steel or similar materials, to enlarge and stiffen the overskirts.
14. *powder:* fine white cosmetic applied to the face and skin to lighten them and to conceal scarring caused by e.g. smallpox, and during this period composed of toxic ingredients (e.g. lead, mercury, lye or bleaches), which could result in blood poisoning. By the mid-18th century, use of whitening powders declined, and during the Victorian period, many face powders used zinc oxide to emphasize a more natural ivory colour.

15. *fine arts:* 'the creative arts, including the visual arts, poetry, music, rhetoric, etc., whose products are intended to be appreciated primarily or solely for their aesthetic, imaginative, or intellectual content' (*OED*).
16. *Rookwood:* Raby's pseudonym may call to mind William Harrison Ainsworth's best-selling gothic novel, *Rookwood: A Romance* (1834), which features hidden inheritances and disguised identities.
17. *Commonwealth:* capitalized, the term refers both generally to the period 1649–1660 (also termed the 'Interregnum'), and more technically to two periods within this time. The 'Old Commonwealth' was the republican government of England that existed under the rule of Oliver Cromwell in 1649–1653 ('the Old Commonwealth'), following the execution of King Charles I in 1649. This was followed by a Protectorate that united England, Scotland and Ireland under Cromwell as Lord Protector, the Parliament of which was dissolved in 1659, to be replaced by a new Commonwealth under Cromwell's unpopular son Richard, before the restoration of Charles II in 1660.
18. *William the Third:* Born in the Netherlands, William of Orange was the husband and co-ruler with Queen Mary, his first cousin, of the British Isles, between early 1689 and March 1702. Their predecessor, the Catholic monarch James III of England and Ireland and VII of Scotland, was dethroned and exiled in December 1688, and replaced by his arch-Protestant daughter Mary II (1662–1694) and her husband William III and II (1650–1702). This signalled the so-called Glorious Revolution, which shifted the reign of the British home nations from an absolute to a constitutional monarchy.
19. *supper:* 'The time and style of "supper" varies according to history, geography, and social factors. For much of its history, "supper" was simply the last of three daily meals (breakfast, dinner, and supper), whether constituting the main meal or not.' (*OED*)
20. *parlyvoos:* derogatory term for the French, deriving from the French question: *Parlez-vous français?* (Do you speak French?)
21. *lingo:* language (colloquialism).
22. *Beelzebub:* originally a Philistine deity, but taken to signify an archdemon, or Satan.
23. *chimera:* fantastical, fire-breathing monster of ancient Greek mythology, made up from the parts of other animals (most commonly, a lion's head, a goat's body and a snake's tale). In this context, Edgar uses its more abstract meaning of something so fantastical as to be illusory.
24. *addlepate:* i.e. 'addle-head', '[a] person whose mind is (supposedly) addled; a stupid or contemptible person.' (*OED*)
25. *stoic:* one who represses one's emotions and is indifferent to pleasure or pain, marked by patience; named after the Stoics, a philosophical school founded by Zeno aroind 300 BCE, who were marked by their austere ethical views and practices.
26. *Phantom:* 'A thing (usually with human form) that appears to the sight or other sense, but has no material substance; an apparition, a spectre, a ghost.' (*OED*)
27. *Avaunt:* onward, go on (*OED*).

The Third Drama [Act III]

1. *Esquire:* indicator of gentlemanly status by birth, status or education.
2. *One and eightpence:* one shilling and eight pence (1s 8d). In the pre-decimal era in the United Kingdom, 20 shillings made up one pound, and 12 pennies made up one shilling. According to the www.MeasuringWorth.com website, in 2023 terms, 1s 8d equates to £10.50 in real wages or £78 in labour earnings. While it is difficult to attribute a precise equivalent to standards at the time of preparing this volume, for most of the 19th century one shilling was the typical amount paid to a manual labourer for a day's work.
3. *Captain:* 'In the army: The officer who commands a company of infantry or foot artillery, or a troop of cavalry or horse artillery, ranking between the major and the lieutenant. The grade is the third in order of promotion.' (*OED*)
4. *her Majesty's army of occupation in Burmah:* British colonial rule of Myanmar (Burma) spanned 1824 to 1948, and expanded in the wake of three Anglo-Burmese Wars fought between two expansionist powers in the Indian subcontent: the British Empire and the Konbaung dynasty in 1824–1826, 1852–1853 and 1885. At the time of *The Vampire*, both its composition and setting of Act III, victorious British forces had been in control of parts of what is now NE India, including the southern Burmese regions of Arkhan (Rakhine State) and Tenasserim (Tanintharyal Region). Defeated in the first Anglo-Burmese War forced the Konbaung dynasty to sign a commerical treaty with and to pay a £1 million indemnity to Britain.
5. *conjuror:* magician, often one who specializes in fake miracles or trickery.
6. *£90 a year:* According to www.MeasuringWorth.com website, in 2023 terms, £90 in 1860 would be just over £13,000 (see also II, n. 2, above).
7. *serious:* in the 19th century, the term 'serious' carried religious overtones, suggesting sincere Christian principles. Later, the term accrued derogatory or mocking implications, to suggest excessive or false piety—it is used in this sense by Rees in his account of Mrs Raby.
8. *she found out that she was a lost sheep:* again, Rees mocks the religious association to Jesus's Parable of the Lost Sheep (Matthew 18. 12–14, Luke 15. 3–7), which tells the story of a shepherd who leaves his flock of ninety-nine sheep to find one which has become lost, suggesting the value of redemption.
9. *backgammon:* 17th-century English board game for two players, which comprises two, often hinged tables, with pieces ('tablemen') whose moves are controlled by throwing dice.
10. *toddy:* 'drink typically consisting of whisky or other spirit, (hot) water, sugar or honey, and sometimes lemon or spices, often considered warming, soothing, or restorative' (*OED*).
11. *imps*: children of the Devil, small demons.
12. *post-horses:* horses kept at an inn or a post-house, for the use by riders carrying the mail or for hire by general travellers.
13. *wrestled with my worser part:* The concept of spiritual wrestling in Christian belief can be traced to the Old Testament, when Jacob wrestles with a stranger who is revealed to be God. He renames Jacob 'Israel', 'because you have struggled with God and with humans and have overcome' (Genesis 32. 28).
14. *wandering in the wilderness of iniquity:* see Numbers 14. 33–34: 'And your children shall wander in the wilderness forty years, and bear your whoredoms, until your carcases be wasted in the wilderness. After the number of the days in

which ye searched the land, even forty days, each day for a year, shall ye bear your iniquities, even forty years, and ye shall know my breach of promise.' The use of such terms was often linked in the 19th century to evangelical Anglicans and Presbyterians: hence, it is being used by Mrs Raby as a kind of religious idiolect that demonstrates her misguided zealotry.
15. *abjured*: rejected or repudiated.
16. *Babel of abomination*: The Tower of Babel was linked to blasphemy and heresy in the Bible, and is used allusively by Mrs Raby to suggest a heretical world; likewise, by 'abomination' she suggests something spiritually destestable or disgusting.
17. *coffer*: chest or strong-box, in which coins or treasures are kept.
18. *bottle imp*: according to German folklore, an evil spirit or demon living in a bottle; such a creature appears in the Friedrich de la Motte-Fouqué's tale 'Galgenmännlein' (1810), which Robert Louis Stevenson adapted into the Hawaiian-set 'The Bottle Imp' in 1891. Here, Rees is using it whimsically in his reference to alcohol, 'the demon drink'.
19. *Hollands—two hundred years in a bottle:* the Dutch *jenever*, a liquor made from fermented malt mixed with juniper berries, which originated in the Netherlands, Belgium and nearby nations; once introduced into England in the early 17th century, this formed the basis of gin and was popularized following the accession of William III of Orange during the Glorious Revolution of 1688 (see II, n. 18, above).
20. *Glasslyn:* Glaslyn (Welsh for 'blue lake') is a lake in the eastern flanks of Snowdon, approximately 2000 ft (600 m) above sea-level; according to Welsh folklore, the mortally wounded King Arthur had his sword Excalibur thrown into Glaslyn.
21. *Henry VII:* Born in Pembroke Castle, Pembrokeshire in SW Wales, in 1457, Henry Tudor seized the English crown by defeating Richard III at the Battle of Bosworth Field in 1485. He reigned as King of England and Lord of Ireland from this point to his death in 1509, and founded the Tudor dynasty, which included Henry VIII, Edward VI, Mary I and Elizabeth I, spanning 1485 to 1603.
22. *Llandwrog:* coastal village in Gwynedd, NW Wales, approximately 10 miles (16 km) west of Snowdon; the name means 'The Church of St Twrog', a 6th-century Welsh saint.
23. *Jetsam and flotsam:* odds and ends, bits and pieces, random items; taken from the legal terms 'jetsam' (wreckage or cargo of a ship found floating on the surface of the sea) and 'flotsam' (goods washed ashore that have been either discarded or thrown overboard from a ship in distress).
24. *what ruffians those Middle Age barons were:* the barons of medieval England were notorious for their unruly and often combative relationships with each other and the monarch, using legal, political and martial means to effect their aims.
25. *sarcophagus tomb:* coffin made of stone, often embellished with carvings, sculptures or inscriptions.
26. *Tableau:* 'A representation of the action at some stage in a play (esp. a critical one), created by the actors suddenly holding their positions. Also as a stage direction' (*OED*).

THE PHANTOM

Act I

1. *brawn*: 'The muscle or flesh of animals as food' (*OED*).
2. *Snowdon*: Set within Snowdonia, North Wales, Snowdon (*Yr Wyddfa* in Welsh) is the tallest mountain in Wales and the highest in the British Isles below the Scottish highlands, standing at 3560 ft (1085 m).
3. *Colonel*: superior officer of a regiment (since the 17th century, the largest permanent unit in the British Army), whether of infantry or cavalry; the Colonel ranks below General and above Lieutenant Colonel.

   Peveril: A ruin by the late 16th century, Peveril Castle overlooks the village of Castleton in Derbyshire, was built at least as early as 1086. It was named for William Peverel (d. 1114), a favourite, and reputedly the natural son, of William the Conqueror. The name 'Peverel' allegedly derives from the Latin *puerulus* (small boy) or *piper* (pepper), according to J. R. Planché's *The Conqueror and his Companions*, 2 vols (London: Tinsley Brothers, 1874), II, 258–75. The name and castle famously feature in the title of Sir Walter Scott's longest novel, *Peveril of the Peak* (1823), which is set during the Restoration period, with most of the action taking place in 1678.
4. *Royal Horse*: Royal Regiment of the Horse Guards was a cavalry unit initially formed in 1650 under the orders of Oliver Cromwell by Sir Arthur Haselrigge, and transformed into the Earl of Oxford's Regiment following the restoration of King Charles II in 1660.
5. *pensioners*: hired soldiers or mercenaries.
6. *Puritan*: member of the austere English Protestant sect from the late 16th and 17th centuries, who sought to complete the reformation of the Anglican Church to remove any crypto-Catholic elements of church practice, which they considered corrupt or unscriptural. The Puritans were associated strongly with the Parliamentary faction during the English Civil War (see n. 8, below).
7. *Captain*: 'In the army: The officer who commands a company of infantry or foot artillery, or a troop of cavalry or horse artillery, ranking between the major and the lieutenant. The grade is the third in order of promotion.' (*OED*)
8. *Roundheads hung the Cavaliers*: Roundheads supported the victorious Parliamentary faction during the English Civil War (1642–1651), who favoured constitutional over absolute monarchy. 'Roundhead' was originally a pejorative term, applied to the Parliamentarians because many of them wore their hair cropped close. They were opposed by the Royalist faction titled Cavaliers, who favoured absolute monarchy and supported the cause of the Stuart monarchs. The term, derived from the French *chevalier* (horseman), was used also pejoratively by their Roundhead opponents. During the mid-17th century, Wales was divided by the Cavalier and Roundhead factions.
9. *every dog has his day*: old proverb popularized by Shakespeare in *Hamlet*, v.1—'"The cat will mew, and dog will have his day"'—indicating that everyone will achieve success at some point in their lives.
10. *Llanberis*: village in Gwynedd, NW Wales, at the foot of Snowdon (see I, n. 2, above); the name is Welsh for 'The Church of St Peris', an early Christian saint, possibly from the 6th century.

11. *troop of horse:* cavalry.
12. *King's highway:* 'the King's (also Queen's) highway: the public road network, regarded as being under royal protection; (esp. in early use) a specific road regarded as belonging to that network.' (*OED*)
13. *hostler:* groom at an inn, who tends to horses.
14. *shanty:* cabin or hut, often poorly built.
15. *thousand pounds:* According to www.MeasuringWorth.com website, in 2023 terms, £1000 in 1645 would be just over £210,000.
16. *guinea:* English gold coin with a value of £1 1s, which circulated between 1663 and 1813; also, a sum of money equivalent to this amount. A guinea would be worth £160 in 2023.
17. *rapier:* 'A long, thin, sharp-pointed sword designed chiefly for thrusting. Originally, in the early 16th cent., a light sword or small-sword worn by gentlemen with ordinary dress and used in self-defence or for the settlement of quarrels, etc. (as opposed to the heavier sword used in battle). Hence developing, in later use, into a long sharp sword suitable esp. for duelling or fencing.' (*OED*)
18. *cypher:* symbolic character or marker.
19. *supper:* 'The time and style of "supper" varies according to history, geography, and social factors. For much of its history, "supper" was simply the last of three daily meals (breakfast, dinner, and supper), whether constituting the main meal or not.' (*OED*)
20. *booby:* 'A childish, foolish, inept, or blundering person; (also) (chiefly English regional) a person (esp. a child) who cries readily, a crybaby. Now colloquial.' Its early use was apparently associated with Welsh English in particular (*OED*).
21. *Bohemia:* region in Central Europe, bordered by Austria to the south, Germany to the west, Poland to the northeast and Slovakia to the southeast. Bohemia was first a duchy of Great Moravia (c. 870–1198), before being subsumed as part of the Holy Roman Empire (1198–1806), the Habsburg monarchy (1526–1804), the Austrian Empire (1804–1867) and finally Austria–Hungary (1867–1918); between 1918 and 1989, the westernmost region of Czechoslovakia; and since 1993, the largest region in the modern-day Czech Republic.
22. *phantom:* 'A thing (usually with human form) that appears to the sight or other sense, but has no material substance; an apparition, a spectre, a ghost.' (*OED*)
23. *the fiend:* the Devil.
24. *recruits:* replenishes the substance or essence of a thing by the addition of fresh material; now rare (*OED*).
25. *bumper of Burgundy:* cup, filled to the brim, with wine from the Burgundy region of eastern France, typically dry reds made from pinot noir grapes or whites from chardonnay grapes.
26. *King Charles:* Born in 1600, Charles I was the son of James VI of Scotland and I of England (1566–1625), whom he succeeded as the second Stuart King of England, Scotland and Ireland from 1625 until his execution by beheading in 1649, during the English Civil War (1642–1651).
27. *Cromwell:* Oliver Cromwell (1599–1658) was a politician and soldier, who led the Parliamentary faction during the English Civil War. Following the execution of King Charles I (for which he advocated) in January 1649, Cromwell governed as Lord Protector of the Commonwealth until his death in 1658.
28. *fratricide:* someone who has killed one's brother(s).
29. *Of all the birds...side by side:* untraced; likely a creation of Boucicault.

30. *corse:* corpse.
31. *work calcium up:* Quicklime, or calcium oxide, was heated with an oxyhydrogen flame to light up important actors and scenes in theatres; a screw would raise or lower the quicklime—in this case Boucicault wanted the top of Snowdon 'in the limelight' (*OED*).

Act Two—Hall in Raby Castle
1. *valises:* travelling cases or portmanteaux, often made of leather and able to be carried by hand.
2. *Corporal. Full Corporal:* non-commissioned officer in the military, one rank below a sergeant, often in charge of a squad.
3. *Flanders:* region in modern-day northern Belgium, primarily made up of Dutch speakers (Flemings); its official capital is Brussels.
4. *a lout, a bumpkin, a clod:* all terms indicating an ill-mannered, awkward person, often associated with rural background.
5. *Dominie:* schoolmaster or teacher (Scottish)
6. *necromancy:* magical practices focused on communicating with and raising the dead.
7. *Principia Demonia by Duns Scotus:* this purported treatise by John Duns Scotus (c. 1265/66–1308), a Franciscan priest and Catholic theologian, does not exist., and is likely a invention by Boucicault. Indeed, he also created a similar book in the Samuel French version: Dr Dee's *Dictionary of Necromancy*, drawing on the reputation for occultism and alchemy attached to the John Dee (1527–1608/09), an advisor to Elizabeth I. It is not known why he felt in 1873 that Duns Scotus was a better model than Dr Dee in 1856—perhaps it just sounded more exotic.
8. *Black Craft:* blanket reference to occult practices, witchcraft and black magic.
9. *Ghouls, Djinns, Bogles, Vampires:* supernatural and malevolent beings, made up of undead (ghouls, vampires), spirits (djinns) and phantoms (bogles).
10. *Christian advice to young people about to marry:* Conduct books with a strong Christian message were popular throughout the 18th and 19th centuries, and offered guidance to young people on how to conduct themselves as they entered society as young adults. Classic examples of this genre include James Fordyce's *Sermons to Young Women* (1765) and *Addresses to Young Men* (1777), John Gregory's *A Father's Legacy to his Daughters* (1773) and Hannah More's *Strictures on the Modern System of Female Education* (1799), all of which continued to be published well into the second half of the 19th century.
11. *Chiefly known in Germany:* The vampire (*der Vampyr*) was a regular haunter of Germanic folklore and European myth, where the creature was also known in Romania as *nosferatu* or *strigoi*, as *vurdulac* and *upyr* in Russia, and as *vrykolakas* in Greece.
12. *parlor:* 'In a manor house, [...] a smaller room separate from the main hall, reserved for private conversation or conference.' (*OED*)
13. *charlatan:* trickster or con-artist.
14. *Je triumphe:* I triumph (French).
15. *Quae:* PB-P inserts this word in pencil in what seems to be an attempt to splice together several languages for dramatic effect, and although it is ungrammatical his possible intended effect was an ejaculation like 'What!'
16. *Eureka:* I have found it!—a phrase said to have been uttered by the ancient Greek philospher and mathematician Archimedes (*c.* 287–*c.* 212 BCE).

17. *platoon of infantry*: 'Originally: a small body of foot soldiers, detached from a larger body and operating as an organized unit, esp. to fire in volleys (now historical). Now: any of various subdivisions of a company of soldiers, esp. infantry; spec. one forming a tactical unit that is commanded by a subaltern or lieutenant and divided into three sections.' (*OED*)
18. *poignard*: small, thin dagger.